A preacher?

Richard was downright shocked to discover that he had been attracted—even for one devastating heartbeat—to this woman. She was absolutely off-limits to a man with his love 'em and leave 'em philosophy, the only kind of philosophy a man with his kind of wandering life-style could have.

He took one long, lingering look at the woman preaching so sincerely about tolerance for sinners and vowed with some regret that that look would be his last.

A preacher for heaven's sakes! Obviously his well-honed antenna for trouble had been seriously on the blink. Well, it was fully operational now, and nothing—*nothing*—would get him within a hundred yards of this particular woman again.

Dear Reader,

Welcome to Silhouette Special Edition...welcome to romance.

That telltale sign of falling leaves signals that autumn has arrived and so have heartwarming books to take you into the season.

Two exciting series from veteran authors continue in the month of September. Christine Rimmer's THE JONES GANG returns with *A Home for the Hunter*. And the Rogue River is once again the exciting setting for Laurie Paige's WILD RIVER series in *A River To Cross*.

This month, our THAT SPECIAL WOMAN! is Anna Louise Perkins, a courageous woman who rises to the challenge of bringing love and happiness to the man of her dreams. You'll meet her in award-winning author Sherryl Woods's *The Parson's Waiting*.

Also in September, don't miss *Rancher's Heaven* from Robin Elliott, *Miracle Child* by Kayla Daniels and *Family Connections,* a debut book in Silhouette Special Edition by author Judith Yates.

I hope you enjoy this book, and all of the stories to come!

Sincerely,

Tara Gavin
Senior Editor

Please address questions and book requests to:
Silhouette Reader Service
U.S.: 3010 Walden Ave., P.O. Box 1325, Buffalo, NY 14269
Canadian: P.O. Box 609, Fort Erie, Ont. L2A 5X3

SHERRYL WOODS

THE PARSON'S WAITING

Silhouette®

SPECIAL ▼ EDITION®

Published by Silhouette Books
America's Publisher of Contemporary Romance

SILHOUETTE BOOKS

ISBN 0-373-09907-X

THE PARSON'S WAITING

Copyright © 1994 by Sherryl Woods

Printed in U.S.A.

SHERRYL WOODS

lives by the ocean, which, she says, provides daily inspiration for the romance in her soul. She further explains that her years as a television critic taught her about steamy plots and humor; her years as a travel editor took her to exotic locations; and her years as a crummy weekend tennis player taught her to stick with what she enjoyed most—writing. "What better way is there," Sherryl asks, "to combine all that experience than by creating romantic stories?"

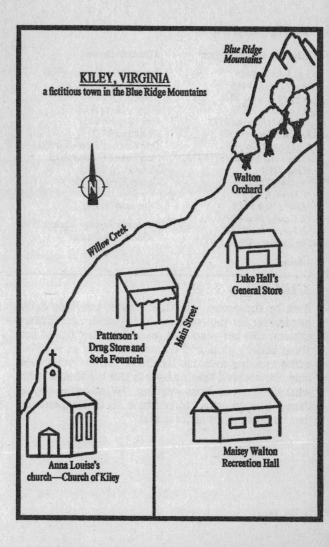

KILEY, VIRGINIA
a fictitious town in the Blue Ridge Mountains

Blue Ridge
Mountains

Willow Creek

Walton
Orchard

Luke Hall's
General Store

Patterson's
Drug Store and
Soda Fountain

Main Street

Anna Louise's
church—Church of Kiley

Maisey Walton
Recreation Hall

Chapter One

Richard Walton stood atop the hillside in Kiley, Virginia, and looked out over his grandmother's apple orchards and beyond to the Shenandoah Valley. For as far as the eye could see there was nothing remarkable on the horizon, just green treetops against a crystal-clear blue sky. He drew in a deep breath of the cool morning air with its hint of the approaching fall and waited for some sort of serenity to steal over him.

Wasn't that why people retreated to godforsaken places in the mountains? Wasn't there supposed to be something in the eternal stillness, in the quiet shifting of the seasons that gave a man peace of mind? So where the hell was it? he wondered irritably.

Coffee cup in hand, he leaned against a post on the front porch of the white clapboard house that had been in his family for four generations and waited impatiently for the place to work its healing magic.

Nothing. Just as it always had, the quiet got on his nerves worse than bullets flying past his ear. And Lord knows he'd had enough of that in the past few years to be able to make the comparison. Even here, where the noisiest thing around was Nate Dorsey's rusty old pickup, he could still hear the thunder of bombs exploding in Iraq, the shelling in the streets of Bosnia, the sniper fire in Somalia.

But as chilling as those sounds had been, they were nothing compared to the cries of starving children, the screams of tortured women. He still woke up some nights in a cold sweat, hearing those godawful moans of anguish. He'd known in his gut that for every one of the children he reported rescued by UN troops or Red Cross workers, for every one of the women whose stories of daring escapes he wrote about for his Washington, D.C., newspaper, there were hundreds or thousands more that no one could save.

For nearly ten years he had been highly paid to report from the world's hellholes. Bloody civil wars, famine and strife were the lifeblood of a foreign correspondent known for his willingness to go anywhere, to brave any danger for the sake of an illuminating interview and a front-page byline. There was little in the way of human depravity that Richard Walton hadn't witnessed. He seriously doubted that an orchardful of apple trees and a lungful of fresh air were going to wash away memories that he hadn't been able to blot out with some of the world's best liquor or a few spectacular, memorable nights of steamy passion.

Sipping the strong coffee he'd grown accustomed to drinking to stay awake during endless hours in the field and even more exhausting hours at his laptop computer, he wondered just how long he'd be able to tolerate the quiet. Hopefully it would be long enough.

He thought of his grandmother, Maisey Walton, whose fragile heart was finally showing signs of slowing down after nearly eighty years. Only Maisey could have drawn him home again.

Not that she'd asked. Maisey knew that he hadn't been able to leave this town with its small-minded people and bitter memories fast enough. She'd sent him off to college with her blessing and she'd proudly kept a scrapbook of clippings from the Washington paper that had eventually hired him to report on the world's trouble spots. She'd told him last night, though, that she hadn't read most of them.

"You've got an eye for detail and a vivid style that makes those horrible things come alive," she'd said. "I can't sleep nights when I've read one of your stories. I shed too many tears for all of that senseless suffering."

Of course, to his way of thinking that was high praise. That was just the effect Richard had hoped to have on readers. He'd wanted people to know what it was like in those distant, terrible places. He'd wanted their discomfort to become a rallying cry for change.

But over the past nine years, if he'd learned nothing else, he'd learned that change was slow in coming, even when all the world's forces for good were intent on making it happen. Mankind seemed to have a boundless capacity for doing harm, but very little understanding of how to do good. That knowledge had made his stories hard-hitting and relentless. It had also turned his heart cold and cynical.

Maybe it was time for a break, time to use up all that vacation time he'd accumulated with his long, uninterrupted stretches on assignments that had other reporters bailing out after weeks. He was finally willing to admit that he was very close to a bad case of burnout.

That alone wouldn't have brought him back to the States, though. His grandmother had done that. Hearing Maisey's voice turning increasingly frail, even when her words had been stubborn, had worried him into taking an extended leave from the newspaper. He owed her for taking him in after his parents had died. He owed her even more for letting him go.

He'd vowed to stay in this crummy little pinpoint on the map through fall when the apples would be picked and when, with any luck, his grandmother's health would be a bit stronger. He had no doubt that there would be another big story to tempt him then. There were always hot spots and too few reporters willing to risk their necks to cover the stories the way they needed to be covered.

Finishing his coffee, he took the cup inside, rinsed it and left it on the old-fashioned porcelain drainboard. If he was going to help out around here, it was time to get started. He needed to walk through the orchards and get a fix on what had to be done first. Maisey had sold off some of the land when keeping up with the acres of apple trees had gotten to be too much. But she'd been adamant about holding on to a few acres for him, declaring stubbornly that one day he might see this place as a refuge. There were enough trees left, their branches heavy with bright red fruit, for Maisey to make her locally famous pies and cobblers all through winter, plus extra to provide her with a small income from sales down at Luke Hall's general store. She'd tended those remaining trees with loving care.

The rest of the property hadn't fared as well, though. The barn, which had once housed Maisey's tired old mare Lucy and Richard's first cantankerous pony, was empty now. The white paint and green trim that had once matched the house had peeled so badly that the barn was mostly the soft gray shade of weathered wood. He doubted he needed a horse, but he vowed to give the barn a fresh coat of paint one of these days. Maybe it would be a symbol of hope for his grandmother. It was no wonder she was feeling so decrepit when everything around her was falling into a sorry state of disrepair.

He'd noticed the same thing in the house. Even though the rooms smelled of lemon oil and the sturdy antique furniture gleamed from weekly polishing, the wallpaper was the same fading rose pattern that had already been old when he'd been a boy. It was time for a change. He resolved to take Maisey shopping for new paint and wallpaper in Charlottesville before the end of the week. Maybe his prejudice was showing again, but he doubted the hardware store in Kiley carried anything that hadn't been on the shelves since the turn of the century.

His thoughts were still on changes to be made to the house when he finally reached the first dwarfed trees in the orchard, trees that had been pruned back for a century or more to keep the apples low to the ground for easier harvesting that wouldn't damage the fruit. The scent of apple blossoms was long past, but he imagined he could smell them anyway. In reality, though, where the blooms had been back in the spring, the branches were now loaded with nearly ripe apples. A few were actually ready for picking.

He reached up and plucked one to sample, rubbing it against his denim-clad leg until the red skin was polished to a shine. Just as he was about to take a bite, he caught a glimpse of color in a tree in the heart of the orchard. Attuned by years of self-protective instincts to paying strict attention to anything that seemed out of place, he moved cautiously toward that bright, unexpected patch of turquoise.

It was probably nothing more than a kid stealing apples, but Richard used a fair amount of care as he quietly approached the intruder. Slipping past the last row of trees, he suddenly came to an amazed stop. He felt a little like Adam must have felt coming upon Eve in the Garden of Eden.

The turquoise he'd spotted from a distance turned out to be a T-shirt worn atop a pair of shorts that weren't exactly skimpy, but which did show off an intriguing amount of bare, shapely leg. He wondered how anyone so innocently sensuous had wound up in Kiley, Virginia. The woman's topknot of red hair had tumbled loose, falling in provocative waves that hid her face. Her bare feet, unadorned by nail polish, were braced against the tree trunk as she clung to a branch with one arm and stretched to reach an elusive apple with the other. Despite her awkward position in the tree, her face, when he finally caught a glimpse of it, bore an expression of radiant serenity.

Richard was entranced. It had been a long time since he'd met anyone who looked so thoroughly, delightfully carefree.

"Is there something special about that particular apple?" he asked in a lazy, interested voice.

The woman's grip on the branch slipped and she started to topple headfirst toward the ground. Fortunately for both of them, she wasn't all that far off the ground and Richard had lightning-quick reflexes. He caught her and held her close, absolutely captivated by the flecks of gold in eyes the exact shade of warm brandy. His heart, which he could have sworn had turned to ice years ago, suddenly seemed not just to have thawed, but to have turned capable of pumping hot blood fast and furiously through his veins.

Maybe he'd just been too long without a woman in his arms. Thinking back to his recent last days overseas, though, he dismissed that. More likely, it was just the unexpected discovery of someone with such an intriguing look of wantonness and innocence in a place where he'd least expected it. It felt something like finding a wildflower stubbornly blooming in a field where soldiers had died.

"So," he said softly, "tell me about the lure of that particular apple, when there's a whole orchard filled with choices. Did it have anything to do with its being the least obtainable?"

She smiled and her whole face seemed to light up. "There is something about a challenge that I can't resist," she admitted.

"I suppose that makes us kindred spirits, then. In which case we should properly introduce ourselves. I'm Richard Walton."

"I know. Maisey told me you were coming home." Her gaze held his, hers thoughtful. "She's missed you, you know."

Richard listened for a judgmental note in her voice, but it wasn't there. It was just a statement of fact. He matched it with the same even tone. "I've missed her, too."

The woman in his arms nodded in satisfaction. "Good. Now suppose you put me down," she said briskly.

He shook his head. "Not until you tell me your name and what you were doing snitching my grandmother's apples."

"Planning to have me arrested?"

"Persuade me I shouldn't."

"It seems like a lot of trouble for one apple, which, I would like to point out, I never did reach."

"How do I know you don't have a whole bushel basket filled with them hidden away behind another tree?"

"Trust me, thievery wouldn't do a lot for my reputation," she said with a dry note that puzzled him. "Besides, Maisey told me I could pick all the apples I want."

"I only have your word for that," he said, reluctant to let her go even though it was entirely likely that Maisey had given her permission to plunder the orchard at will. It had been far too long since he'd met anyone whose expression radiated such unabashed joy. He felt a little like he was basking in the first rays of sunshine after a long, gray winter. This woman, not the peace and quiet, might be exactly what he needed to heal his battered psyche. If she happened to be as adventurous as he hoped, she would certainly brighten his stay in Kiley.

"I'm baking a pie for the church bazaar," she said, as if invoking the mention of church should prove her good intentions.

"When is this bazaar?" he asked skeptically.

"Saturday afternoon. Maisey also told me you didn't have a lot of trust left in your heart," she informed him. "This is Kiley, not Bosnia or Somalia or any of those other places you've been. You can let down your guard."

The reminder broke the magical mood. "Hey, I grew up here, remember? Just being Kiley isn't a great recommendation. People may not be shooting each other with guns, but they're just as capable of destroying a man," he said bitterly, finally lowering her to her feet.

Her eyes immediately turned sad and she reached up and touched his face with a feathery-light brush of her fingers. "What is it?"

"Nothing. I've got to get back to the house and check on Maisey. No doubt I'll be seeing you around." Ignoring her puzzled expression, he turned his back on her then and walked away.

"No doubt," she called after him.

Five minutes earlier and the promise would have sparked anticipation. Now, though, with unexpected memories of all the things that had made him want to leave Kiley in the first place suddenly crowding in again, Richard felt only the same dull ache he'd carried in his chest for the past ten years.

Anna Louise Perkins spent an inordinate amount of time on Saturday afternoon gazing up the road toward the Walton place. To her regret, her distraction was noticed by half the people attending the church bazaar, including Maisey Walton. Maisey might be nearing eighty, but she had a sharp mind and observant blue eyes that sparkled with intelligence. She also had the heart of a matchmaker. Anna Louise had been a tough challenge for her, refusing to cast a second look at any of the single men in town.

"What did you think of my grandson?" Maisey inquired casually, her gaze following the direction of Anna Louise's.

"How did you know we'd met?"

"He mentioned something about finding a woman up in one of my apple trees. That could only have been you. Everyone else is satisfied with picking what they can reach from the ground." She patted Anna Louise's hand. "Stop peering up the road like that. He won't be coming. Said he wanted no part of the town. He just came home to look after me."

"But you're here," Anna Louise noted. "How did you get down the hill? You didn't walk, did you?"

"Young lady, I've been walking up and down that hill for the better part of eighty years. I suppose one more trip won't kill me."

"Maisey, you know what Doc Benson told you. You're not as young as you once were. Your heart...."

"Oh, fiddle-faddle. I've had a few pains. I'm an old woman. And I'd rather go out doing the things I've always done than wasting away in that old house, bored to tears."

Anna Louise embraced the woman she'd come to think of as her own relation. "Regardless, you are not to walk home. I'll drive you whenever you're ready to go. Got that?"

Maisey smiled tolerantly. "Whatever you say, dear."

Anna Louise regarded her suspiciously. Such easy acquiescence was out of character. "What are you up to, Maisey Walton?"

"Me?" the older woman replied with exaggerated innocence. "I'm not the one looking for excuses to sneak another peek at my grandson."

"I hope you remember to pray for forgiveness to-morrow," Anna Louise cautioned, trying not to laugh. "That tart tongue of yours has a touch of the devil behind it."

"You let me worry about my soul, young lady. You've got plenty of other work to do. Now go on about your business. I think I'm going to go over to that kissing booth where that handsome young doctor is puckering up for a dollar. Now *that* will be a test of the shape my old heart is in."

Laughing, Anna Louise watched Maisey march determinedly across the church grounds, her aim straight for the line in front of the kissing booth. When the idea for such a booth had been proposed, there had been some commotion at the church. It had been resolved when Doc Benson, who belonged to a different congregation, had agreed to run it.

She studied Jonathan Benson and wondered why she wasn't the least bit tempted to join the line. He was handsome enough with his warm brown eyes and dark brown hair. He'd been smart enough to get his medical school degree from Harvard and to serve an internship at Johns Hopkins. And he had a dry sense of humor that she could appreciate. But there was none of that chemistry all the romantic fairy tales talked about. She liked Jonathan Benson enough to share a cup of tea with him occasionally, but that was it. She definitely had no desire to go over and plunk down a dollar for a kiss, not even for a good cause.

Not that it would have been an appropriate thing for her to do, anyway. The church's congregation would have been scandalized. She wondered how they'd feel if they knew the thoughts that had scampered through her head when Richard Walton had held her in his arms a few days earlier.

With his hard, trim body, his too long hair that looked as if it had been kissed by sunlight, and his haunted eyes, he was the kind of man that stirred a woman's sympathy and senses. Anna Louise had learned long ago that that particular combination was deadly. A purely sexy man was one thing, but one who looked as if he needed loving was downright dangerous. She'd decided on the spot that Richard Walton was definitely such a man.

In general, her life in Kiley was an open book, but her thoroughly feminine reaction to Maisey's grandson was definitely something she didn't intend to share with a soul. Unfortunately, Maisey seemed to have guessed. Anna Louise wondered what it would take to persuade her to keep her suspicions to herself. Knowing Maisey's sense of mischief and her powerful desire to play matchmaker, Anna Louise expected the price would be high.

"Young man, I want you out of that bed right this instant," Maisey stated firmly from the doorway to Richard's room.

He bolted upright, stared at Maisey through sleep-blurred eyes, groaned, rolled over and buried his head under a pillow. Maybe she would give up and go away.

"Richard!"

"It's the middle of the night," he protested.

"I don't know why you're so tired. I'm the one who spent the whole afternoon at the bazaar yesterday. I haven't had that much excitement in a long while. That nice Doc Benson is quite a kisser."

That brought his head up. "You were kissing a doctor?" He tried to recall a physician his grandmother's age. He came up blank. "Who is he?"

"He's very handsome," she said slyly. "And not a day over forty. Quite a catch."

Richard felt a headache coming on. Where had he gotten the idea that his grandmother's health was failing? Obviously the real problem was that she was delusional. "You and some forty-year-old doctor were making out down at the church yesterday?"

"It was worth every penny I paid him for it, too," she said and sashayed off, leaving behind the familiar scent of her lilac perfume.

Richard bolted out of bed and managed to dress in less than five minutes. He roared into the kitchen. "Grandmother, what the devil is going on? Did I understand you to say you were paying some man for sex?"

"Not sex," she said indignantly. "A few kisses." She grinned at him. "It was for a good cause. The church needs a new roof."

Richard sank down and buried his head in his hands. "I don't believe this. Why would you do this to me?"

"Do what?"

He scowled at her. "Never mind."

"Go get your good shirt on. We're due at church in a half hour."

Going to church was not the way Richard had planned to spend his morning. If that woman he'd met in the orchard was baking pies for the church bazaar, then she was also likely to be sitting there in the middle of the congregation. Bolts of lightning were reserved for men who thought the kinds of wicked thoughts she inspired, especially while sitting in church. Besides, he hadn't exactly experienced a lot in the last few years to reinforce the spiritual teachings of his childhood.

"Sorry. I think I'll do some work around here."

"And how am I supposed to get there?" she demanded, making an obvious attempt to sound pitiful.

Richard wasn't taken in by the act. "You walked down that hill on your own yesterday," he reminded her. He'd argued with her about it at the time, but she'd been adamant that she would not be dependent on him or anyone else to get around.

She clasped a hand to her chest. "I'm not so sure I could make it again today. I think it was too much for me."

He didn't buy the convenient excuse for a minute. "I think all that kissing was probably what did you in," he countered dryly. He finally relented. "Okay, I'll drive you down and pick you up."

"Oh, for goodness' sakes, if you're going to go to all that trouble, you might as well stay. The service only lasts an hour."

He frowned. "Did you ever know General Patton?"

"Can't say as I did."

"I'm surprised. You two would have had a lot in common." He sighed and left the table without even one good jolt of coffee. "I'll be ready in a minute."

He went back upstairs and put on a suit and tie he'd bought years before for a friend's wedding. He hadn't had a lot of occasion to wear it since. In fact, it had stayed right here in his old closet, along with the other mementos of his past.

Downstairs, Maisey nodded approvingly. "Very handsome."

"Better looking than the doctor?"

"Definitely."

Not fifteen minutes later they were at the church. Richard managed to avoid giving more than a nod here and there to folks who recognized him. He slid into a pew beside Maisey and settled back to wait out the hour by deciding which project around the house to tackle first. He stood when nudged, sat down with everyone else, all the while paying little or no attention to anything going on.

Then he heard *her* voice, low and mellow and seductive as hell. There wasn't a doubt in his mind that it was the woman from the orchard. And she seemed to be starting the sermon.

Richard's gaze shot up and, sure enough, there she was, standing square behind the lectern, looking as innocent as a newborn babe, in a gray dress with a prim little lace collar. That dress looked as if it had come from Maisey's closet about forty years ago. Sedate was the kindest word he could think of to describe it. She still looked delectable...and official. His mouth fell open.

Maisey tucked her arm through his and leaned close. "We've been needing someone with a spark of energy for years now. The church hasn't been the same since she came. Isn't she something?"

"What on earth is she doing up there?" he asked, still not willing to acknowledge the logical answer. He had to hear it spelled out in plain English and even then he knew he wasn't going to like it.

"Why, she's the preacher, of course."

Even though he'd expected it, the announcement left him speechless. He waited for that bolt of lightning from the heavens to strike him down for the lascivious thoughts he'd had about her. When he could finally find his tongue, he said in a stunned tone, "But she's a woman."

"Well, of course she is," his grandmother said, as if that were no more surprising than the choir leading off with "Rock of Ages."

Richard suddenly had the disturbing sensation that Kiley, Virginia, had skipped the twentieth century and leapt straight into the twenty-first. He was shaken by the discovery that his perceptions of his old hometown were at odds with reality.

More importantly, he was downright shocked to discover that he had been attracted—even for one devastating heartbeat—to a woman who was absolutely off limits to a man with his love 'em and leave 'em philosophy, the only kind of philosophy a man with his kind of wandering life-style could have.

He took one long, lingering look at the woman preaching so sincerely about tolerance for sinners and vowed with some regret that that look would be his last.

A preacher, for heaven's sake! Obviously his well-honed antenna for trouble had been seriously on the blink in that orchard. Well, it was fully operational now and nothing—*nothing*—would get him within a hundred yards of this particular woman again.

Chapter Two

"So, Richard, what did you think of our new pastor?" Maisey asked when the service was over.

She didn't wait for an answer, which was just as well, given Richard's inability to form a coherent thought at the moment.

"Isn't she something?" Maisey enthused, as if she were doing public relations for a political candidate... or a prospective bride. "Anna Louise does know how to give a rousing sermon. Of course, there are some in town who don't think a woman has any business leading a congregation, but she'll win them over eventually."

"That explains why half the pews were empty," Richard said, mostly to himself. He'd thought maybe it was because too many of the men were attracted to the preacher and had started worrying about those same lightning bolts that weighed on his mind. "Do they give her a hard time?"

"Some do, but Anna Louise pays 'em no mind. The girl has more gumption than a raccoon after picnic leavings. She's known what she wanted since she was a little bitty thing. Grew up with a real sense of purpose, a calling, you might say." She slanted a sly look at him. "A woman like that could make a man's life mighty interesting, don't you think?"

Richard ignored the broad hint, but his opinion of Miss Anna Louise Perkins shifted dangerously toward approval again. Anyone who stood up to the small-minded folks of Kiley had his full support. Her career might make him jittery on several counts, but none had a thing to do with any judgments about women as preachers. As a matter of fact, he considered himself to be very liberated. He'd always believed women had a right to pursue any job their brains and strength enabled them to hold. He'd met some tough, courageous females in his travels, women he admired more than he could say. Some carried guns. Some carried notebooks or TV cameras. Some wore stethoscopes. All had been singlemindedly dedicated to what they were doing.

To his deep regret, however, he had to concede that his personal plans for Anna Louise, formed in that orchard a few days ago, had suffered a serious setback. In fact, he could think of two very solid reasons for avoiding her like the water in some Third World country.

First, she was bound to be the kind of woman who'd have certain expectations of a man. In her position as a preacher, already precarious because of her gender, she couldn't afford to go around indulging in casual flings with a man who was just passing through town.

Second, the last thing he needed in his life was some do-gooder who believed that people were decent and kind. He could cite any number of occasions in the past nine years when he'd seen proof of just the opposite. In fact, he had his own bylined newspaper clippings and the accompanying horrifying photographs to back it up. For purely intellectual purposes, maybe someday he'd ask Anna Louise how she explained a God who allowed those terrible things to happen. Given that quiet, serene aura she had about her, maybe that was something Anna Louise had never given any thought to, but Richard had. He hadn't liked the answers he'd come up with.

It seemed, however, that despite his resolve not even to think about the town's newest preacher, his grandmother had other ideas. All the way back up the hill, Maisey continued to sing Anna Louise's praises. In fact, Richard thought he knew more about the woman after that five-minute drive than he had about most of the women he'd slept with since leaving Kiley. It kept him uncomfortably aware of her and of the instantaneous, heart-pounding attraction he'd felt when they met.

According to Maisey, Anna Louise was twenty-nine. She'd been born in Tennessee. She had three older sisters and uncompromising, dedicated parents who'd been at the forefront of the fight for civil rights in the South. She'd been a miracle baby, born prematurely at barely three pounds. That early battle to live had turned her into a scrapper and taught her from her first days that miracles were possible.

"Not a day went by that her parents didn't thank God for the blessing of her survival," Maisey concluded. "I have to admit I think we're just as blessed that she decided to come here to Kiley. She was sent here just to fill in, but the majority of the congregation voted right off to keep her. To my way of thinking, it was God's plan that sent her here and we had no right to object. Of course, there were those who disagreed so vehemently that they left. Good riddance, I say."

"I suppose," Richard mumbled. Then to his grandmother's obvious regret, he went off to change his clothes, rather than listen to more high praise of the most unavailable woman in Kiley, Virginia for a man with his particular designs on her.

When he came back into the kitchen, his grandmother was frying chicken and boiling potatoes to mash. Green beans simmered with some bacon for seasoning. A cookie tray of homemade yeast rolls was ready for the oven. Richard sniffed the air appreciatively, then waved a finger under his grandmother's nose.

"Does your doctor know this is the sort of meal you fix?" he scolded. "I haven't seen this much cholesterol in one place since you took me to that all-you-can-eat buffet in Charlottesville after my high school graduation.''

She frowned at him. "This is the same Sunday dinner I've been eating my whole life,'' she informed him.

"Which could explain why you're having problems with your heart."

"Fiddle-faddle. My heart's just plain old. It doesn't have a thing to do with what I eat for Sunday dinner."

He glanced at the table and saw that three places had been set with the best china. "Is your new boyfriend joining us?" he teased. "Now that you've shared a few kisses with the doc, are you hoping to reel him in with your cooking?"

"Stop that nonsense, Richard Walton," she said, smacking his hand as he reached for a chunk of apple coated with cinnamon and sugar. "And stay out of those. They're for the cobbler. It's Anna Louise's favorite. Yours, too, as I recall."

His heart seemed to skid to a stop. "Anna Louise is coming for dinner?"

"She'll be here as soon as she finishes up at the church."

Richard saw his good intentions going up in smoke. Proximity with Anna Louise would not do a lot for his resolve. The wires connecting his body and his brain tended to get crossed. His head might be shouting "Hands Off," but other parts of his anatomy clearly hadn't gotten the message.

"I know what you're up to," he told Maisey, hoping to ward off any plans she might have of throwing him into daily contact with the preacher for whatever devious purpose she had in mind.

"And what would that be?" she inquired innocently.

He refused even to mention anything having to do with marriage. "It's too late to try saving my wretched soul," he said instead.

"Maybe I'm more worried about my own," his grandmother retorted, but there was an unmistakable and worrisome glimmer of amusement in her eyes.

He made up his mind to flee while he could. "Bye," he said, heading out the back door with one last look of regret at the meal he'd miss.

"Where are you going? Dinner's almost ready."

"I'm not hungry."

"Fiddle-faddle," she said emphatically, clearly unconvinced. She shot a penetrating look at him. "Running scared?"

"Just running," he said as he left the house for his own protection.

Unfortunately, his grandmother had never been easily dissuaded from one of her schemes and Anna Louise apparently had the tracking skills of a hound dog. She found him down by Willow Creek. He'd discovered his old fishing pole in the barn, dug up a few worms and was contentedly resting against a tree with his line dangling in the creek. He hadn't had a nibble in the past hour, but for the moment he was perfectly content to sit back in the shade and wait.

"Catch anything?"

The cheerful inquiry interrupted his pretense at dozing. He'd seen her coming and had hoped Anna Louise would take one look at his sleeping form and leave him in peace. Obviously she was no less easily dissuaded from a mission than Maisey. At the moment, he didn't view that as an attribute.

"Not yet," he told her, shoving his hat back to slant a look up at her. She'd changed out of that prim little dress into linen slacks and a cool-looking blouse that bared her slender arms. He absolutely refused to check out how those slacks fit over her trim little behind. "Thought you'd be sitting down to fried chicken by now."

"Without you? That wouldn't be polite."

"I told Maisey I wasn't hungry."

Anna Louise looked skeptical. "Gee, it must have slipped her mind."

"Conveniently," he said dryly. "One thing about Maisey, she has a very selective memory."

"I don't suppose this sudden fascination with fishing had anything to do with my coming to dinner."

She didn't seem especially troubled by the possibility. If anything, she looked fascinated. "Why would I let you chase me off?" he asked testily.

"If I had to hazard a guess, I'd say panic."

It was all Richard could do to keep from choking. "Why would I panic?"

"Why, indeed?"

His gaze narrowed. "You're not hoping to get me to confess my sins, are you?"

Her burst of laughter rippled through the summer air. "While I'm sure that would be titillating, I don't have any need to drum up business. I'm in the habit of waiting for people to come to me when they want to talk about their transgressions."

"From what I hear, you're the last person some people in town would come to," he said, and watched as her expression clouded over. Whatever she might have told Maisey about ignoring the people who disapproved of her, their opinions clearly hurt.

"No matter what profession a person is in, it's impossible to please everybody," she said pragmatically. "Just ask Luke Hall how folks have been treating him since he stopped carrying five different brands of corn flakes because he was running out of shelf space."

"But old Luke has the hide of an elephant," Richard observed. "Something tells me you don't."

She shot him a troubled look, as if she hadn't expected him to be able to read her so easily. "How'd we get on this, anyway?" she demanded, sounding flustered. "I came down here to haul you back to Sunday dinner. I don't know about you, but I'm starved. A rousing sermon always makes me hungry."

Richard recognized a lost cause. Anna Louise wasn't about to go back to the house alone and face Maisey's wrath. "Let's go," he agreed, getting to his feet in one lithe movement. He struck off ahead of her, then turned back. His gaze pinned on hers, he said quietly, "Give 'em hell, Anna Louise. That's what the folks around here deserve."

He caught a glimpse of her startled expression before he picked up his pace and moved on.

* * *

Over Maisey's crisp, fried chicken, buttery mashed potatoes and gravy, green beans and apple cobbler, Richard struggled with his baser instincts. It took everything in him to keep his eyes on his plate and his thoughts in line. It had to be some sort of divine test. If it was, he was failing miserably. All he could think about was Anna Louise's pale as milk skin. All he could wonder about was whether she felt like silk or satin, whether she'd be warm or cool to his touch. Why was it man's perverse nature to desire what he couldn't have?

He couldn't for the life of him reconcile what Anna Louise did for a living with the observant young woman who kept them laughing at her outrageous stories about Luke Hall down at the general store in town, and his lazy trio of good-for-nothing sons. Naturally, Anna Louise seemed to think those boys had the potential to be saints, particularly young Jeremy, who, at eighteen, was already making plans to be married. Richard could have told her stories about those three hellions, but he didn't. No point in disillusioning her, if she couldn't see what was plain as day. Jeremy was the instigator of most of their mischief. Jeremy married? Richard couldn't picture it. Nine times out of ten, a boy who got married at eighteen hadn't been able to think of any other way to persuade his girl into bed. Maybe parsons had to turn a blind eye to facts like that.

Right on through dessert, Richard kept waiting for Anna Louise to offer to save his sorry soul, but either she didn't feel it was worth saving or she was storing up the offer for another occasion. He was almost disappointed not to have the chance to tell her what she could do with her plans for his eternal salvation.

Anna Louise honestly didn't know what to make of Richard Walton. She'd heard about Maisey Walton's grandson, the renegade journalist who defied death by chasing stories into places no other journalist would dare to go. He was every bit as bitter and cynical as she would expect a man to be after witnessing the atrocities he had seen.

And yet she knew that no grandson of Maisey's could grow up without being instilled with her values and generosity of spirit. She wondered what it would take to wipe that jaded look from his eyes and restore the sense of joy he must have felt as a child growing up in this beautiful, serene place.

At least Richard hadn't turned out to be one of those people who thought she didn't belong behind the pulpit. Her very own pastor back in Tennessee didn't hold with women preaching, even though she'd been encouraged to attend Sunday school and take part in youth leadership activities. It seemed a line had been drawn at the front of the church and she wasn't allowed to step over it.

Fortunately her parents had understood her calling and had encouraged her to follow her chosen path, no matter how difficult it might be. Some of her own cousins, however, had been appalled and had wasted no opportunity to tell her so. As for the men in her classes at seminary, most of them had felt it their duty to show her that she didn't belong. It was amazing how selective they could be in their reading of Scripture, picking only passages which seemed to disapprove of women in the pulpit. She had quietly gone about the business of proving them wrong, by becoming better educated, a better preacher, and a more tolerant person than any of them. She also had her own Bible passages to counter all their claims.

Being asked by the congregation to become the fulltime pastor of the church here in Kiley had been the sweetest, most satisfying moment of her life. It had made all of the years of struggling, all the tests of faith worthwhile.

Clearly, though, Richard Walton had been taken aback to discover her profession. There had been an unmistakable difference between the way he'd treated her the day they'd met and the way he'd acted during dinner. On that first day he had reacted to her and she to him, their responses as natural as could be between two people whose hormones were intact.

Now, though, there was a distance, a caution that hadn't been there before. It wasn't the first time she'd experienced such a reaction. Some men seemed to fear eternal damnation if they dared even to ask her out. Up until now she had always been able to shrug it off, partly because she'd had her career to keep her occupied. It was challenge enough without adding romance to her life.

Quicker than the blink of an eye, Richard Walton had changed that. For the first time in her life, she thought she knew the real meaning of temptation. She had to admit she was oddly disgruntled that a man who reportedly feared nothing suddenly seemed to fear even having a conversation with her.

Had it been any other man, she might have convinced herself to forget about it, but this was Maisey's grandson. Maisey clearly worshiped him, and Anna Louise loved Maisey. There was no question that she and Richard Walton would be thrown together more than might be wise, given the sparks that had been there when they'd first met.

But, she thought irritably, if today had been anything to go by, he seemed perfectly capable of resisting the temptation.

Surely she had every bit as much willpower as he did, she told herself sternly. Just in case, though, she vowed to pray very hard that the next time she saw him she would find him to be no more attractive than a toad.

Chapter Three

Unfortunately, Anna Louise's fervent prayers went unanswered. When she ran into Richard Walton inside Patterson's Drugstore and Soda Fountain first thing on Monday morning, her traitorous heart skipped a beat. He had the bluest eyes she'd ever seen, with little crinkles at the corners from laughing or from looking into the sun. She preferred to think it was the former, even though she'd barely seen his mouth curve into a smile. Surely at some point in his life, he'd found things to laugh about.

"Miss Perkins," he said formally.

There was no mistaking his reluctance to acknowledge her existence. He'd cast one desperate look around as if there might be another exit that wouldn't necessitate going past her.

"Mr. Walton," she said, matching his prim demeanor and wishing she could think of some way to tease him out of it. She would give almost anything to see that spark of purely masculine interest back in his eyes again. She had almost given up hope that any man in Kiley would ever look at her like that. She—or her profession, to be perfectly accurate—intimidated most men, even after they got to know her. She sighed at the loss of a potentially fascinating relationship.

She was so absorbed in her own regrets that she missed Richard's shifting stance and his uncomfortable determination to offer an unneeded explanation for his presence in town.

"I just came in to pick up some medicine for Maisey," he said.

Instantly, worry crowded out this stupid game they seemed to be playing, a game at which she was obviously thoroughly inept. A woman who had been determined to get through seminary despite all the odds had little time left to perfect the art of flirting. Besides, it would have been considered unseemly. She'd spent a lot of effort taming anything in her outgoing personality that others might view as a wild streak.

"Is Maisey feeling okay?" she asked at once.

"She claims she is, but I noticed she wasn't moving quite so fast this morning. And she barely touched her breakfast. Hopefully it's nothing more than her arthritis acting up. It turned cool overnight." His gaze met hers and skidded away. He was staring at a point beyond her left shoulder—probably at the exciting display of Ace bandages—when he added, "Anyway, thanks for asking."

Anna Louise made a quick decision. "Perhaps I should come back to the house with you. Sometimes she's too stubborn to call the doctor when she's feeling poorly."

"It's not your problem," he said curtly. "I'll call the doctor, if she needs him."

Anna Louise didn't have a lot of patience for people who wouldn't accept help when it was offered. "And how will you tell? Do you have a medical degree I don't know about?"

"Do you?" he countered.

"No, but I know Maisey."

He stiffened visibly. "She's *my* grandmother. Are you suggesting I don't know her as well as you do?"

"Her health has been failing steadily for the past few years," she shot back without thinking about how it might hurt him. "You haven't been around, so, yes, I guess I am saying that I know more about it than you do." She glared at him. "Is that really the point?"

He looked downright bemused by the attack. He probably thought pastors weren't subject to the same flare-ups of temper that afflicted other people. Anna Louise almost felt sorry for him and not just because he'd underestimated her. A guilty conscience sometimes had a way of taking a person by surprise.

She looked into his eyes and suddenly relented. However rotten his attitude was toward most people, he clearly loved Maisey and was bound to be worried by the decline in her health. After all, it had been enough to bring him home when nothing else ever had.

"How about a cup of coffee?" she suggested impulsively.

His gaze narrowed suspiciously as if he were trying to figure out some ulterior motive for the offer. "I thought you were so damned determined to get up to the house to check on Maisey."

She clung tenaciously to her last thread of patience. "Five minutes won't make any difference. Think of this as an olive branch. It's clear you and I have gotten off on the wrong foot this morning. I don't want Maisey to worry about the tension between us. She'll pick up on it right away."

He sighed and some of the stiffness eased out of his shoulders. "You're right about that. Okay, a cup of coffee sounds good."

They sat down and Tucker Patterson brought the coffee to the table, along with two pieces of homemade coffee cake they hadn't ordered. The old pharmacist grinned at Anna Louise.

"I don't want to hear any of your dieting nonsense, young lady. You need your energy if you're going to keep up with all you've got to do around here. Saving sinners can take a toll on a person. Leastways, that's what my son is always telling me."

She glanced over and caught Richard grinning. His smile was everything she had imagined, warm and devastatingly attractive.

"And me?" he said to Tucker. "You trying to give my energy a boost?"

"I doubt your energy needs it. Unless you've changed, you can turn around and eat five minutes after your last full meal. When you and Orville were boys, I had to put the two of you on the payroll around here just to break even."

Anna Louise chuckled at Richard's indignant expression, fascinated by the obviously fond byplay between him and Tucker. "Isn't that a little like leaving the foxes guarding the henhouse?" she asked.

Tucker's eyes twinkled behind his rimless glasses. "Sure was, but I paid them in food they'd have eaten anyway. At least I wound up with free help." He winked at her. "Now you two enjoy yourselves. Good to see you back, Richard. Hope you'll be around for a while. I know Orville will be mighty glad to see you."

When he'd gone back behind the counter, Anna Louise bought some time by tasting her pecan coffee cake and taking a few swallows of coffee.

"So you and Orville Patterson grew up together," she said finally, after it became obvious that Richard had no intention of getting the conversational ball rolling.

He nodded. "You know him?"

Anna Louise considered her reply carefully. She and Tucker Patterson's son were not on the best of terms. In fact, he was leading the crusade to get her thrown out of her church, had been from the day she'd been voted in. His father, thankfully, didn't seem to share his bias against women preachers. In fact, Tucker obstinately sat in the front pew of her church every single Sunday just because he knew it gave his stiff-necked son hives. Unfortunately, just in the last two months Orville had gained support from two new pastors in the region.

"He's the pastor over in Jasper Junction," she said finally. "We meet on occasion."

Richard shook his head in wonder. "Old Orville is a preacher? Well, I'll be damned."

She grinned at his amazement. "Not what you expected of him?"

"Actually, I thought he'd go straight from juvenile hall to prison."

Fascinated, she leaned forward. "Exactly what mischief did you and Orville used to get into?"

"By today's standards it wouldn't even warrant a slap on the wrist, but back then we were regarded as troublesome," he admitted.

"Come on, tell," she encouraged. "What did you do?"

"Why the fascination with our childhood pranks?"

Anna Louise wasn't prepared to admit that her motive wasn't entirely pure. She figured one of these days she could probably use all the ammunition she could get to fight the narrow-minded man who'd sworn to see her thrown out of the Kiley church or die trying. "Let's just say I always like to know the character of the people I'm dealing with."

He shot her a puzzled look. "Are you talking about me now or Orville?"

"Both," she said candidly. "Though I assure you the reasons are very different."

He leaned forward intently, a sudden glimmer of pure mischief crossing his face. That look reminded Anna Louise of Maisey and made her like him all the more. In a way, she suddenly felt as if she knew him.

"Do tell," he said.

She shook her head. "You first," she insisted.

"Okay, then," he agreed, but he took his time about getting on with it. He stirred another teaspoon of sugar into his already sweetened coffee and took a long sip, before leveling a serious look at her. "Keep in mind, though, that Orville was always the ringleader. I was merely an innocent he led astray."

Though his tone was sober, she caught the amusement lurking in his eyes. "Right," she said dryly. "Talk."

"Well, now, let's see." He drummed his fingers on the table as if he was considering which tale to tell first. The one he chose brought a smile to his lips. "I suppose the height of our glory as Kiley's bad boys was the time we stole Mabel Hartley's girdle from the clothesline and paraded it around town like a flag."

"That's not so bad," Anna Louise said, trying— and failing—to hold back a chuckle. She doubted, however, that Mabel had the sense of humor needed to excuse the act.

"You don't understand," he said, sounding offended that she hadn't given the misdeed enough credit. "Mabel was chagrined. She was convinced that everyone in town thought her fine figure was purely natural."

Anna Louise practically choked on her coffee. "Excuse me, but she weighs nearly two hundred pounds now. What did she weigh back then?"

"At least that," Richard confirmed. "It was a helluva girdle. I'd say that sucker could have tucked in the sides of a freighter."

Anna Louise laughed out loud at the image, but what made her even happier was the expression of pure devilment on Richard's face. She was right about the laughter. It transformed him. The hard angles of his face softened. His eyes lit up. For an instant there was no trace of the hard, bitter man who'd seen too much of death and destruction around the world.

"What else?" she prodded, just to keep the mood alive. "Nobody goes to jail for stealing a girdle and embarrassing one of the town's matrons."

"They do if her husband is the sheriff, which he was back then."

"Oh, my."

"Orville and I spent two whole hours in a jail cell until Maisey and Tucker came storming through the door to rescue us. Actually I credit Tucker with that. I think Maisey was inclined to leave us there. She was very sympathetic to poor Mabel." He shook his head, an expression of wonder crossing his face. "I can't recall the last time I thought about that."

"You've had other things on your mind the past few years."

"That's part of it, I suppose."

"Only part?"

He shrugged. "The good memories of Kiley were few and far between after that summer. It wasn't all that difficult to forget they'd happened at all."

Anna Louise was taken aback by the renewed bitterness in his voice and by its apparent cause. "What happened to make you hate this place so much?"

His gaze lifted to meet hers. The spark had gone out of his eyes, leaving them dulled with pain again.

"Small town, small people. Let's just leave it at that," he said in his typically cryptic way. He picked up the bag of medicine and shoved it in his pocket. "I'd better be getting back to Maisey."

Anna Louise blamed herself for the sudden shift in his mood, the renewal of the tension between them. For a fleeting moment he'd seemed almost happy. Then he had plunged back into that dark antagonism that she had foolishly attributed entirely to his experiences overseas. Now it seemed obvious that Richard Walton's discontent had begun right here in Kiley a long, long time ago. Given that, she wondered if he'd stick around long enough for her to figure out what made him tick. She found herself oddly disappointed by the thought that he might not.

Richard's long strides took him up the side of the mountain in less than half an hour. The day had quickly turned hot and humid, a last reminder of summer before autumn's chill arrived for good. Sweat broke out on his forehead and streaked down his back. At least he could blame the heat for leaving him feeling restless and irritable. Chances were, though, that was only part of the explanation. Anna Louise was the bigger part of it.

He was glad that she hadn't followed him from Patterson's. He'd seen the questioning expression in her eyes and knew that she'd be pestering him for explanations he had no intention of giving. Even if she weren't a preacher, she would be the kind of woman who'd always want to make things right. She'd never be able to accept that there were some things it was impossible for a man to forgive and forget. Even Maisey didn't fully understand this hold the past had on him and she had lived through the grief and anger with him.

He deliberately pushed the old memories aside, along with the more recent nagging little sparks of attraction Anna Louise set off in him. Sitting across from her in that old-fashioned booth with its red vinyl cushions and black Formica-topped table, he'd forgotten for a moment that she wasn't just any woman. Her sassy tongue had fueled the confusion. He did love a woman with a temper and Anna Louise clearly had spirit to spare. His hormones had reacted without a pittance of consideration for her profession. Apparently the hands-off message hadn't gotten through, even though he'd spent a restless night repeating it again and again.

When he should have been thinking about Anna Louise speaking from that pulpit, he kept seeing her stretching for that apple in Maisey's orchard. The two images were not compatible. One was a solemn reminder of what happened to sinners. The other was provocative, sweet temptation.

Damn his sorry hide, he had always been drawn to danger, and Anna Louise surely was that. This time he'd been so sure that he'd have the good sense to resist. After this morning, though, he had his doubts, which made it all the more important that he not stick around Kiley a second longer than necessary.

He was walking up the dirt road leading to the house when a car breezed past him without even slowing. His heartbeat accelerated. Maisey! Had she gotten worse while he'd been gone? Had the doctor been called? Only at the last second as the car sent up a trail of dust did he catch the sheen of the driver's red hair.

So, he thought grimly, Anna Louise had followed him, after all. He should have known being left behind wouldn't deter her.

Only the thought of Maisey's medicine tucked in his pocket kept him from taking his time going inside. He did linger by the kitchen window for a bit, though. The two of them were seated at the table, thick as thieves. If his grandmother was still feeling under the weather, it didn't show. She was pouring a cup of tea for her guest and demanding to know what was going on in town.

"Did you run into Richard?" she asked, her tone all innocence, but obviously zeroing in on what fascinated her the most.

"At the drugstore," Anna Louise said.

"I thought you might. You're usually there about this time every day," she said.

Richard bit back a chuckle. The old sneak! He'd wondered why she'd been in such a rush to shoo him out the door, insisting that she had to have her medicine right away, when it was clear to him now she was just fine.

"I wonder why he didn't come back up here with you?" she said to Anna Louise.

"He probably had another errand," Anna Louise replied. "I did see him walking along the lane up to the house. He should be here soon."

A disapproving frown settled over Maisey's face. Or maybe it was just disappointment, Richard decided. She probably hated the fact that the two of them weren't falling in with her plans.

"You didn't offer him a lift?" she chided. "Why, I'm surprised at you, Anna Louise."

"I suspect he preferred having the time to himself."

Richard stepped inside. "Or perhaps he just has more sense than to ride with a woman who drives like a maniac," he chimed in from the doorway. He crossed the room in two strides, leaned down and kissed Maisey, then put her medicine on the table. He glanced at Anna Louise. "Are you in such a hurry to meet your Maker?"

"I'm surprised at you. For a man who dodges gunfire without blinking an eye, you seem to lack a sense of adventure," Anna Louise accused with a good-humored smile. "Besides, I've never gotten so much as a scratch from an accident, whereas I hear you have a whole collection of scars from your intrepid lifestyle."

He couldn't help imagining how much fun it would be to explore her skin inch by delectable inch just to be sure she was telling the truth about the lack of scratches from her reckless driving. Since following up on that idea was definitely off limits, he simply said, "Touché. Now if you two will excuse me, I'm going to take a survey of the barn to see what it will take to fix it up."

At the screen door, he paused. "Maisey, if you're feeling up to it this afternoon, I thought we could drive over to Charlottesville to pick up some paint for the barn and maybe some new wallpaper for in here."

Maisey gave him an inscrutable look. "I think the trip would be a little too much for me," she said, suddenly sounding weary.

Richard regarded her suspiciously. Despite her tone, she didn't look the least bit tired. She obviously had some reason for feigning exhaustion and he was willing to bet he knew what it was.

His suspicions were confirmed, when she added, "Why don't you take Anna Louise? She knows my taste as well as anybody. She can pick out the wallpaper."

Anna Louise glanced at him. She looked about as dismayed by the prospect of being confined in a car with him for hours as he was.

"Really, Maisey, this is something that should be your choice," she said hurriedly. "I'm sure Richard can bring back samples, if you don't want to go along with him.''

His grandmother's chin set stubbornly. ''Then that'll mean a second trip. What's the use of that? No, Anna Louise, I'd like you to pick something out, something cheerful. You have the time, don't you? You always take Mondays off.''

Clearly beaten by Maisey's clever scheming, Anna Louise sighed. ''I have the time.''

''Well, then, that's settled,'' Maisey said.

If Richard had had a grain of sense, he would have worried about the triumphant note in her voice. Instead he just nodded, deciding he might as well make the best of it. ''We'll go right after lunch.''

''Fine,'' Anna Louise agreed. ''I'll be ready.''

''Perfect,'' Maisey said enthusiastically. ''Why don't you stay there for dinner and a movie? It'll be a nice break for both of you. How often do you get a chance to eat in a nice restaurant?''

''Maisey, I just got home,'' Richard protested. ''I don't need a break and I've spent the last ten years eating in restaurants.''

''And I really should be back to do...'' Anna Louise's voice trailed off. Finally, she added weakly, ''Chores. I have a lot of chores I always leave for Monday.''

''Fiddle-faddle,'' Maisey said dismissively. ''Those chores will still be waiting next Monday. When opportunity comes knocking, you should take advantage of it.''

"Opportunity," Anna Louise repeated with evident nervousness. Her gaze was pinned worriedly on Richard.

He knew exactly how she felt. He hadn't been this uneasy going into Iraq the day before the bombs had started dropping. His boss had called *that* an opportunity, too.

Chapter Four

Self-preservation made Richard long to toot the horn when he got to Anna Louise's just after twelve-thirty. He did not want to go inside the parsonage, which he remembered all too well as a grim, sterile place from Pastor Flynn's day. He didn't like envisioning Anna Louise in that kind of environment. She deserved color and light to go with her personality.

Unfortunately, Maisey had pounded strong Southern manners into him from an early age. He parked the car and went to the front door, then waited for Anna Louise to answer his knock.

"Come on in," she hollered from the depths of the house. "The door's open."

Richard turned the knob, infuriated by her irresponsibility. "Have you lost your mind?" he shouted as he stepped into the foyer. "I could have been a mass murderer."

"But you're not, are you?" she said calmly, wiping her hands on a dish towel as she came toward him from the hallway that he recalled led to the kitchen.

"You had no way of knowing that," he observed. "You couldn't even see it was me from back there."

She faced him unflinchingly. "Now let's just think about this a minute," she said reasonably. "If you were a mass murderer, would a flimsy old lock have stopped you?"

He scowled at her. "No, but—"

"Forget it," she told him with a grin. "You can't win."

"I'm not trying to win," he snapped in frustration. "I'm trying to save your neck."

"If I'm not worried about it, why should you be?"

She had him there. "Fine. Get yourself killed," he said. "Are you ready?"

"Let me put this back in the kitchen and I'll be right with you."

While she was gone, he glanced around for the first time. Something had happened to the parsonage. And he had no doubts at all that Anna Louise was responsible for the changes. It was no wonder Maisey trusted her to pick out wallpaper. With probably no decent budget for decorating, she had turned the little house from a dark, dreary place into a sunny, cheerful environment.

The walls had been painted a pale shade of yellow that reminded him of daffodils. The woodwork was white. The stiff old furniture he remembered had been replaced with over-stuffed chairs and a sofa covered in yellow and white pinstripes. Astonishingly healthy plants in pots of every size and shape sat on every available surface. Where heavy drapes had once blocked out the light, now sheer curtains let it in. The transformation was astonishing.

"I can see from your expression this isn't the way you remember it," she said when she returned, her purse in hand.

"Far from it," he said. "This suits you."

"Thanks. It's taken me five years to get it the way I wanted it, but the downstairs is finally done. Someday I'll get to the bedrooms. I can't wait to get rid of Pastor Flynn's hard, punishing mattress."

It was the wrong thing to say. Richard immediately pictured her in bed, disheveled from lovemaking, pliant in his arms. Dear heavenly days, it was going to be a very long afternoon.

"Let's go," he said gruffly.

She shot a puzzled look at him, but she didn't argue. Maybe she'd mentioned that damned mattress deliberately, knowing it would disconcert him.

Thanks to that, all of Richard's journalistic skills deserted him on the drive to Charlottesville. He'd always thought there wasn't a human being on the face of the earth, power broker or pauper, that he couldn't interview. In a normal social setting that skill translated into easy, casual conversation. Talking to Anna Louise was proving to be the exception.

All of the normal questions a man might ask a woman in whom he was interested seemed too intimate, too likely to lead them off on a dangerous conversational path. Of course, that might have had something to do with his inability to remain the slightest bit objective in her presence. Every masculine instinct called for his usual flirtatious, live-for-the-moment approach to an attractive woman. He suspected there were special places in hell for men who flirted with pastors.

Anna Louise wasn't helping matters any. She seemed perfectly content with the silence in the car, perfectly engrossed in the passing scenery. That only made him more determined to find some safe way to draw her attention back to him. A discussion of the weather, aside from being boring and predictable, seemed unlikely to elicit the sort of conversation he wanted. Asking how a woman had ended up a preacher struck him as a mite too touchy, given the objections some people apparently had to her choice. Finally conceding he was at a loss, he settled into his own grim silence.

"Tell me what it was like," she said eventually.

He glanced over at her. She was still staring out the window. "What was what like?"

"Being a correspondent in all those places."

"You don't want to know."

"Yes, I do."

"Why?"

"Because..." She turned to face him, a frown puckering her brow. "Because I need to understand."

"Me or life?" he asked dryly.

"Both, I suppose."

He still wasn't sure why this was suddenly so important to her, but he summed it up succinctly with a phrase that applied equally to every single place he'd been assigned. "It was hell."

"If it was so terrible, why did you do it? Are you one of those people who thrive on danger?"

"I suppose that's part of it. Being challenged just to stay alive, struggling to get the story and get it right, all of it makes every moment vivid and memorable. You cling to those moments because you never know when the next one might be your last. You know with every fiber that you're living life, not letting it pass you by."

"Did you need that kind of intensity after leaving Kiley?"

He grinned. "Let's face it, staying alive in Kiley is not a problem. The only thing that'll kill you here is the boredom."

"I wonder if that's all there was to it," she said, regarding him with a doubtful expression.

"Meaning?"

"Sometimes people force themselves into dangerous situations out of some sort of death wish. It's the kind of thing someone with low self-esteem might do to get attention, either by succeeding dramatically or getting themselves killed."

Richard might have taken offense, if the suggestion hadn't been so laughable. "Trust me, my self-esteem is intact. All foreign correspondents have egos the size of Texas. We're a rare breed, maybe a little like fire-fighters.''

Anna Louise still didn't look convinced by his glib answers. "There's something more, though, something you're not telling me. Are you sure your motivations were entirely selfish?"

Richard regarded her sharply, startled by her apparent intuitiveness. "What are you suggesting?"

"That maybe you went because you felt someone had to, because you knew the world had to see what was going on if there was going to be any chance at all to make things different." She leveled a look at him. "Maisey showed me some of your articles."

"Really?" Given her own reaction to the vivid contents, he was surprised that Maisey had shared them, especially with someone like Anna Louise, who was probably blind to the extremes of human depravity or whose sensibilities might be offended by the grim reality.

"They were very good," she said quietly. "I felt as if I were right there with you. You made the most complex stories human. I could feel the pain and the anger, the despair, the hunger. You brought all of that alive."

Not knowing how else to respond, he simply said, "Thank you."

"There was something else you did, as well."

"Oh?"

"I wonder if you were even aware of it," she said, her gaze fixed thoughtfully on him. "Somehow I don't think so."

"What do you mean?"

"You also captured that fragile sense of hope that flickered to life in even the most horrific tragedies."

Richard had to admit he was taken aback by the assessment. "Hope?" he said derisively. "There were instances of blind folly, not hope."

She nodded, her expression suddenly sad. "Somehow I thought you'd see it that way. It says a lot about the way you and I view the world, doesn't it? You see the cup half empty. I see it half full. You see the evidence of evil. I see the potential for good. I suppose, though, that it's no wonder you've suffered a crisis of faith, given what you've been through."

She said it as if she felt sorry for him, which only served to infuriate him. "One of us is wearing rose-tinted glasses, Pastor Perkins," he chided.

"And one of us is deserving of pity. I wonder if you even recognize which one that is."

"How do you explain the atrocities?" he demanded. "Surely you have some easy answer, one that's compatible with your beliefs?"

She shook her head. "No, I don't, but just because I don't understand doesn't mean that I have to give up my faith that God has a plan."

"I guess that's where you and I part company," he said grimly.

"Yes, I suppose it is."

She settled back into her seat then, her unhappy gaze returning to the passing landscape. The silence this time was all the more oppressive, because Anna Louise's gentle criticism stung. He tried telling himself that her opinion of his outlook on life didn't matter. *She* was the one whose vision was skewed. Unfortunately, the easy dismissal didn't work as well as it might have only days ago.

Instead he found himself wondering what life would be like if he could view it through her eyes. He found himself hoping against hope that tragedy never caused her to see it as he had. Something told him, though, that in her own quiet way, Anna Louise had the toughness and strength it would take to survive no matter what hand she was dealt.

Anna Louise couldn't imagine what had possessed her to taunt Richard as she had on the drive into Charlottesville. He certainly hadn't given any indication he was looking for an outsider's impression of the choices he'd made in his life. Nor did he seem to care two hoots about his own motivations.

He was clearly a man who'd made certain decisions—for better or worse—and intended to stick by them. The why of it didn't seem to matter much to him. From Anna Louise's perspective, that was incredibly sad. And if there was one thing she despised, it was the tragic waste of a life for no reason at all.

Two things that going against the grain to become a preacher had taught her were patience and the will to fight the odds. If she put her mind to it, surely she could show Richard Walton that living didn't have to necessitate dodging bullets. Maybe she could even prove to him that not everyone in the world was dedicated to doing harm. And from what she'd been able

to discern, that lesson would have to start in Kiley, not
in some far-off place where the politics were Byzan-
tine and strife was the only certainty.

First, though, she had to win him over. Right now
he trusted her about as much as a path through a
minefield. Well, if there was one thing she had going
for her, it was her people skills. She hadn't gotten to
be a pastor without knowing how to get along with
just about everybody, even those who mocked her or
flat-out detested her. She'd even managed to have a
civil conversation with Orville Patterson on one occasion. Only one, but she had viewed it as a start,
which only lent credence to Richard's assessment of
her as nothing more than a cockeyed optimist.

She caught him glancing over at her as they pulled
into the parking lot in front of one of those hardware
superstores. It was right next door to a giant Wal-
Mart.

"There's no need to come with me, if you have
shopping you'd rather be doing," he offered.

"Then which one of us will explain to Maisey that
we don't have any wallpaper?"

"I can choose."

She glanced critically at his blue plaid shirt and olive
green khaki pants. "I don't think so."

"Okay, fine. Suit yourself. But I don't want to
spend the whole damned afternoon in here. If you're
planning to get all fussy over choosing paper, then
we'll just have to take home samples."

Anna Louise rolled her eyes heavenward and prayed
for patience. "I'll lay you odds that I can select a

wallpaper faster than you can settle on paint for the barn.''

His gaze narrowed. "Are you supposed to gamble?"

"Worried about my soul?"

"Just checking."

"It's not gambling if it's a sure thing." Her gaze clashed with his, daring him to back down. "Is it a bet or not?"

"What are the stakes?"

"The winner gets to pick the movie. The loser has to pay."

He nodded. "You're on."

Inside the door of the superstore, they separated like two people charging out of a starting gate. What Anna Louise had failed to mention was that Maisey had shown her at least half a dozen home decorating magazines with pictures of exactly the kind of wallpaper she wanted to redo the house, if she ever had the time. Those very same pictures were currently tucked in her purse.

Not that she needed them. As Maisey had said earlier, Anna Louise knew exactly what Maisey liked, because their tastes were incredibly similar—old-fashioned, bright and cheerful. The only exception had been the subdued stripe in beige, navy blue and burgundy that Maisey had picked out for Richard's room. Anna Louise was tempted to pick out something a little more wicked, just for the pure devilment of it.

She zeroed in on the wallpaper section and began making choices, loading up her cart with the appropriate number of rolls for each room based on the careful measurements Maisey had given her.

A half hour later she was finished. She wheeled the cart over to the paint section, grinning as she spotted Richard engrossed in conversation with a salesclerk. There wasn't so much as a brush or roller in his shopping cart. The young clerk looked as if he were at the end of his rope.

Richard regarded her with an expression that was entirely too smug, given her victory. "Couldn't make up your mind after all, I see," he said, gesturing at the assortment of paper.

"Oh, I made up my mind, all right. I'm through."

"You have six different papers there."

"Exactly. The floral is for the parlor. The soft blue stripe is for the dining room. The yellow and white is for the kitchen. This other stripe is for your room. The old-fashioned pink is for Maisey's and this last one is for the bathroom. I figured we might as well get everything at once." She smiled cheerfully. "Where's the paint?"

He seemed to take her victory in stride. He didn't even try to hide the fact that he hadn't settled on a thing.

"We were just discussing that," he explained. "John here is recommending the white flat outdoor paint that's on sale. I think it makes more sense to go with the more expensive one that has a longer warranty."

Anna Louise bit back a laugh. "You haven't even chosen the brand yet?"

He scowled at her. "It's an important decision."

"Of course it is," she soothed. "We used the more expensive brand on the church last year. It does seem to be withstanding the weather exceptionally well."

Richard nodded. "Then that's it. We'll take that one."

"How much?" the clerk asked, turning a grateful look on Anna Louise.

Richard's gaze flew to the gallon cans. "How much?" he repeated doubtfully. "A couple of gallons, I guess."

"More like five or six, minimum," Anna Louise corrected casually. "We used something like ten to do the church and parsonage. The barn's smaller, but the wood is badly weathered. It'll probably absorb most of the first coat. You'll need two coats."

"Who's doing this job, you or me?" he grumbled.

"You, of course," she said at once. "I was just trying to be helpful. I doubt you've had many opportunities to paint the past few years. I did the parsonage and helped with the church. I enjoy it. It relaxes me."

"Then I'll expect to see you tomorrow morning. Bring along an extra ladder," he suggested.

"Sorry. Church circle is in the morning. The ladies are making quilts to send to AIDS babies in the hospitals around the country."

He regarded her with an amazed expression. "Whose idea was that?"

"Theirs, of course."

"I'll bet," he muttered, but he was regarding her speculatively. "Something tells me you could sweet-talk a person into doing just about anything you had a mind to."

"I'd like to think my powers of persuasion are well-honed," she agreed. "Now, about the trim on the barn. Dark green would look wonderful."

"I was going to paint the whole thing white this time."

Anna Louise shook her head. "Maisey and I saw a green and white barn over toward Orange one day. She commented then on how lovely it was. Said it reminded her of the way her place had been when your grandfather was alive."

A look of resignation on his face, Richard turned to the clerk. "A gallon of green paint, too."

"Forest green, moss green or lime?"

Richard looked to Anna Louise.

"Definitely forest green," she said.

"Is that everything, then?" he inquired dryly.

"I'd say it's enough to keep you busy for the next month."

"Trying to keep me out of trouble, Pastor?"

"I did wonder what mischief you'd get into if left to your own devices," she teased.

The look Richard directed at her sizzled straight through her. She swallowed hard and tried to ignore the sudden leap of her heart.

"You don't want to know, Anna Louise," he said solemnly, his gaze never wavering. "You definitely don't want to know."

Unfortunately, she had a very vivid idea and it scared the tarnation out of her, because she couldn't see herself resisting the way a proper preacher ought to.

Chapter Five

Anna Louise Perkins was certainly full of surprises, Richard decided when he finally allowed himself to recall their last encounter in graphic detail. She had responded physically to his taunts in the middle of the hardware store. There had been no mistaking the glint of fascination sparkling in her eyes, a woman's fascination with a man.

He tallied the evidence—the faint flush in her cheeks, the slight curve of her mouth in what might have been the beginning of a smile. That warning that she didn't want to know what was on his mind was the closest he'd come to one of his flip, flirtatious remarks. Not only hadn't she hauled off and smacked him, she had almost seemed to encourage him with that shy, pleased smile.

Her reaction was all the more disconcerting because he suspected a woman in Anna Louise's position had perfected the art of the withering glance. What he didn't comprehend was why she hadn't directed such a look at him. To his way of thinking, that failure to put him in his place made spending time around her doubly dangerous.

Because the first thing he knew, he'd be testing the limits. It was second nature to him. It had taken all of his willpower to get through dinner and a movie that night without stealing a simple kiss.

Heaven help him if she'd suddenly taken it in her head to test her own limits, as well. She wouldn't be the first woman who had, but surely preachers didn't do things like that, he reassured himself. For all of her outspoken certainty about the goodness of people, Anna Louise had clearly never run across a persuasive man whose intentions weren't purely honorable. If she'd been living as pure a life-style as he imagined, any experimentation would likely send them both up in flames.

He wondered about the quirky sense of fate that had plunked a woman like Anna Louise in his path. Perhaps it was simply some sort of divine test. So far he'd passed, but by the slimmest of margins. Anna Louise might credit everyone with the potential for sainthood, but he knew better, especially about himself.

Over the past few years he had learned to take comfort and passion where he could find it. The women he'd known had shared that terrible sense of desperation that made two people cling to one another through long, lonely, frightening nights without sparing a thought for tomorrow. Anna Louise, to the contrary, was all about tomorrows.

It was fortunate, he told himself as he slapped the first coat of paint on the side of the barn, that she wasn't his type at all. She was bossy, for one thing. Smug, for another. And she was too damned insightful. She'd been able to read him from practically the first moment they'd met. A man needed the comfort of knowing that some of his secrets were safe. With Anna Louise that wasn't likely. If she didn't guess them, she'd wheedle them out of him.

Fortunately he had recognized right off—okay, not in the orchard, but right after he'd seen her behind that pulpit, anyway—that they were about as suited as oil and water. Just as fortunately, she didn't strike him as the sort of woman who was looking for a man to fill in the empty space in her life. She might be looking to add a little spice to her humdrum existence, but the bottom line was that Anna Louise was downright self-contained.

Frankly, he found that to be one of the most disconcerting aspects to her personality. He'd known a lot of independent women in his time, but none had radiated quite the same self-awareness and contentment that Anna Louise projected. He was hard-pressed to define the difference, but he suspected it had something to do with being spiritually centered the way she was. Her faith was strong and, as far as he knew, had never been sorely tested as his had been time and again.

That unshakable faith, of course, was something he didn't expect ever to understand. He had a better chance of grasping quantum physics.

Giving up even a passing attempt at figuring out what made Anna Louise tick, he forced his attention back to painting. He was glad now that Anna Louise had prodded him into buying more paint than he'd thought he needed. The wood was slurping it up faster than he could coat it on. He'd be lucky to get by with two coats at this rate.

While he painted, he kept a wary eye out for Anna Louise. In the two weeks he'd been home she had made a habit of tearing up the lane to the house at least once a day. Most times, she simply waved, then disappeared inside to visit with Maisey. He wasn't sure if they were praying or gossiping in there, but Maisey's spirits were always brighter after one of Anna Louise's visits.

He'd commented on that last night during supper. Maisey's response hadn't been particularly illuminating.

"I've always loved having company, you know that," she'd told him.

"But I get the feeling there's a special bond between you and Anna Louise," he'd prodded. "Is it because she's your pastor?"

"There is that," Maisey admitted. "But mostly I just enjoy her company. She's always cheerful. She has a way of looking at life that brightens my day. I can't tell you how much better I feel after we've had a laugh or two."

Richard had retreated into disgruntled silence after that. He could only recall laughing with Anna Louise on one occasion, when he'd told her about stealing Mabel Hartley's girdle. Most of the time they got off onto some serious self-examination that cut too damn close to the bone.

When he'd realized that he was envious of his own grandmother's easy, comfortable relationship with Anna Louise, he'd completely lost patience with himself and stalked off to bed. But even with his head buried under a pillow, he hadn't been able to keep out the troublesome images of a redheaded woman who could tempt even a saint to sin—and he was definitely no saint.

Now that he thought back to that instant of self-disgust over supper the previous night, he couldn't help remembering something else, as well. Maisey had watched him leave the table with an irritating expression of satisfaction written all over her face. Now, what the hell had that been about?

On the first Friday morning in October, Maisey didn't get out of bed. When Richard went into the kitchen, he found the shades still drawn from the night before and the stove cold. His heart slamming against his chest, he forced himself to walk slowly down the hall to her bedroom.

"Maisey," he called softly as he opened the door.

She was huddled under the blankets, looking lost and even more frail than she had the day before. Her gaze was as sharp as ever, though.

"What's got you in such a tizzy?" she asked irritably.

"Who says I'm in a tizzy?"

"You just busted into my bedroom. Doesn't a woman have the right to sleep a little late once in a while?"

"You never do."

"How would you know?"

The comment stopped him cold. An ache formed in the region of his heart as guilt sliced through him. The ache was all the more painful because Anna Louise had already opened that particular wound.

"You're right. I guess I don't know your habits after all this time." He sat down on the bed and took her hand in his. "I'm sorry. I never meant to stay away so long."

She sighed heavily. "No, I'm the one who's sorry. Just because I'm a mite more tuckered out than usual, I don't have any right to be making you feel guilty for going off and doing what you had to do. I know how you felt about living here in Kiley. From the time your mama and daddy died, you were hell-bent on getting out. I could never blame you for that."

Richard missed most of the apology and ignored the reference to his parents' deaths because his brain had focused almost entirely on Maisey's open admission that she was "tuckered out." It wasn't a phrase she or anyone else had ever used about her as far back as he could recall. Most people commented on her astonishing energy.

He looked her over, searching for some indication that she was pale or feverish. But other than looking a little tired, she didn't seem any worse off than she had since he'd come home. Still, he didn't want to take chances. "Maybe I should get Doc Benson over here."

Maisey immediately looked alarmed. "Why on earth would you want to call him? So he can tell me I'm old? Don't waste the man's time. I'll be fine. I just need to rest a bit. The excitement of the past few weeks is wearing on me. Having you home again has been wonderful, but I've been missing my afternoon cat-naps."

Richard wasn't entirely convinced by the explanation, but he decided to give in for now. He'd just keep a very close eye on her for the rest of the day. "Why don't I fix you breakfast and bring it to you in bed?" he suggested.

"The way you used to on special occasions when you were a boy?" she asked, chuckling.

Richard winced at the memory of those mostly disastrous attempts to please her. "Actually you'll have to take my word that my cooking skills have improved considerably since then. So, how about it?"

She drew the old-fashioned quilt up and settled back against the pillows, clearly pleased by the offer. "Maybe a soft-boiled egg and some toast. Can you manage that?"

"I was hoping for a real challenge, but if an egg and toast are what you want, then that's what you'll have."

He was in the kitchen half an hour later, trying for the third time not to burn the bread in the old manual toaster that Maisey had refused to trade in on a newer pop-up model, when Anna Louise rapped on the screen door and strolled in. She eyed the tray with its bouquet of just-picked marigolds in a jelly jar, the runny egg, which was probably like ice by now, and the nearby discarded pieces of burned toast.

"Looks appetizing," she commented.

"Go to—" he began, and stopped himself just in time.

She grinned and picked up the carton of remaining eggs. "Here, you do another egg and I'll make the toast. I gather Maisey's not feeling well."

"She says she's just tired."

"I suppose she is. First she built up all that anticipation over you coming back and then there was the excitement of having you here and supervising all the work you're doing to fix the place up. She could probably do with a day or two in bed."

He fought the desire to snap at her again for thinking she knew what was best for Maisey. The troubling thing was that she probably did. At least she had echoed what Maisey had just told him herself. He wondered if his grandmother had passed along the same complaint to Anna Louise. He didn't want to ask the next question that came to mind, but he had to. He didn't regret the choices he'd made for his own life, but he hated to think of Maisey living some isolated, lonely existence with her only grandson off roaming the world.

"While I've been gone, has she been locked away up here all alone or has she been getting out?" he asked, trying not to let the depth of his concern show.

To his relief, Anna Louise chuckled. "If you think anyone could keep Maisey tied to this house, then you've misjudged her will. She walks down that hill every Tuesday for church circle and again on Sunday for services. She walks into town most days for the mail, rain or shine. Sometimes on the way back, she'll stop by my place for a cup of tea."

He regarded her in confusion. "She hasn't done any of that since I've been home. Has she suddenly taken a turn for the worse? Damn it, I knew I should have called Doc Benson when I found her still in bed this morning." He started for the phone, but Anna Louise put out a hand to stop him.

"Wait a minute. I doubt she needs a doctor."

"Will you make up your mind? One minute you say she's worn out. The next you're telling me she's sprightly as a woman half her age. Which is it?"

"Maisey is almost eighty," she reminded him. "Naturally she tires more easily than she once did. Yes, it's true that she keeps herself busy, but she also knows how to pace herself. If I had to guess what's going on with her now, I'd say she's laying it on a little thick. I think she's playing possum just a bit in the hope of keeping you around longer."

Richard was bewildered by the apparent need for subterfuge. "But I promised her I'd stay as long as she needs me," he said.

"Exactly. As long as she needs you."

Suddenly all of the other hints of weakness, counterpointed against the high spirits whenever Anna Louise was around, began to make sense. He surmised that the frailty, or at least some of it, had been feigned for his benefit.

"Why that old devil," he muttered, taking things off of the tray and setting them on the table.

"What are you doing now?"

"We're having breakfast. All of us," he added emphatically. "Right here in this kitchen. Forget the soft-boiled egg she asked for. Scramble the eggs, would you? I'll be back in a minute."

He stalked into Maisey's bedroom a moment later and found her reading a magazine, which she hurriedly tried to stuff under her pillow.

"Reading *Playgirl* again?" he inquired.

She scowled at him. "Of course not."

"Then why'd you hide it in such a rush? Afraid I'd discover you're putting on an act?"

"What act?"

He leveled a look at her. "Maisey, how do you feel this morning? The truth."

"I told you. I'm fine," she said defensively.

"Just a little tuckered out?"

"Exactly."

"Anna Louise is in the kitchen."

Her expression brightened at once. "She is? Why didn't you send her in?"

"I told her you were too exhausted for company. She and I will be having breakfast in there."

"Oh." Her voice and her expression went flat.

"You could join us," he suggested casually. "If you're up to it."

She shot him a look of sudden comprehension. There wasn't a hint of guilt on her face, though. "You're entirely too smart for your britches, Richard Walton."

"So they say," he said smugly. "Shall we expect you in a few minutes?"

"I'll be there. Get out the strawberry preserves. They're Anna Louise's favorite."

"I'll make note of that." He grinned at her. "You have all the subtlety of a steamroller, Grandmother."

"Well, somebody has to give a thought to your future. You certainly aren't doing a thing about it. You're never in one place long enough to meet a nice woman, much less court her."

"If you think Anna Louise Perkins is in my future, then it's your mental health we need to be worrying about."

Maisey regarded him complacently. "I guess we'll just see about that, won't we?"

"Grandmother!"

"Oh, hush up, young man. You don't scare me. Now get back to our company."

"Company? To hear you tell it, Anna Louise is practically one of the family."

"If I were you, I'd watch that smart tongue. We'll just see who has the last laugh."

She said it so damned smugly, Richard wondered if he'd make it through breakfast without Maisey getting a proposal on the table on his behalf.

* * *

Anna Louise scrambled a fresh batch of eggs and kept a pile of perfectly browned toast warm in the oven as she listened to the squabbling coming from Maisey's bedroom. She couldn't hear what the two of them were saying, but there was a cheerful, teasing tone to it that pleased her for Maisey's sake. Having Richard home was a real tonic for her, better than any of the medication Doc Benson had prescribed.

She glanced up from the eggs when Richard strolled into the kitchen. "Is she feeling better?"

"The cure was almost instantaneous. She heard you were here."

"She didn't have to get out of bed to visit with me."

"I don't think you were precisely the incentive," he said dryly.

She regarded him quizzically. "Oh?"

"I'm sure it will come as no surprise to you that Maisey has ideas for the two of us. She's not about to miss an opportunity to see how her plans are coming along."

Anna Louise could feel the blood rushing into her cheeks. "You must be mistaken," she said weakly, even though she knew in her heart that Richard was absolutely right. "You and I...we aren't..."

He grinned. "Exactly what I told her. She doesn't seem to be persuaded."

"Maybe I'd better leave before she gets in here," she said, hurriedly spooning the eggs onto a platter and grabbing the toast from the oven. "Everything's ready. You two can just help yourselves. Tell Maisey I'll stop by later."

Richard caught her arm when she would have spun toward the door. "Oh, no, you don't. You're not leaving me alone to explain what I did to run you off."

"But we can't let her go on thinking that something will happen between us. Just imagine how disappointed she'll be if we let her get her hopes up."

"Then we can just sit here over a nice breakfast and explain to her perfectly sensibly that we are wrong for each other. That ought to clear it up so there will be no misunderstandings down the line."

To Anna Louise's deep regret, his matter-of-fact approach to the problem irritated the daylights out of her. Of course, he was right. They had nothing in common. They had no future. But he didn't have to sound so darned pleased about it.

"Well," he prodded, "isn't that the best way to handle it?"

"I suppose."

He gave a little nod of obvious satisfaction. "Good, we're agreed. You can tell her."

Anna Louise regarded him indignantly. "Me? She's *your* grandmother. Besides, it was your idea. Why do I have to tell her?"

"Because she'll listen to you. After all, would a preacher lie?"

Not if she could help it, Anna Louise thought grumpily. She might, however, slug a man, given enough provocation. Richard Walton was unwittingly providing almost enough. In fact, she found his certainty over their unsuitability downright insulting. She could hardly tell him that, though.

"We'll both explain," she finally compromised. "I'll tell her why I could never be interested in a cynical, impossible man like you and you can fill her in on why you object to me."

His gaze narrowed. "Impossible?"

"That's one of the kinder things I can think of to describe you," she shot back, satisfied by the dull red flush in his cheeks. Good, he was almost as irritated as she was.

"You know you're playing with fire, don't you?" he said, his voice suddenly low and entirely too calm.

Anna Louise's stomach flipped over. Still, she kept her gaze even with his. "Am I?"

He took a step closer. Her pulse skittered wildly. Wicked, exciting images tumbled through her mind. He reached toward her. But before his fingers could make contact with her cheek, he lowered his hand and backed away as if he'd sensed the white-hot heat of a flame. Anna Louise's heart pounded so hard she could hear the rush of blood. Then, when she realized there would be no more, the dull ache of disappointment settled in.

"Damn," he muttered under his breath. When he looked at her again, his expression was shaken. "I'll be painting the barn, if Maisey needs me."

"Coward," she said to his retreating back.

He turned and shot her a rueful look. "You'd better be damned glad I am, Pastor Perkins."

The screen door slammed shut behind him.

"Well, phooey," Anna Louise said to his back, wishing she could give voice to a more emphatic curse. The man only called her *Pastor Perkins* when he was trying to point out the differences between them. Whether it was for her benefit or his, she wasn't quite sure.

For reasons she didn't care to examine too closely, she wasn't one bit delighted to discover that Richard Walton had the willpower to resist her. She regretted more than she could say that his hand hadn't quite caressed her cheek, that he hadn't dared a single kiss.

Knowing that, she had to wonder exactly which one of them was the bigger fool.

Chapter Six

Anna Louise's mood was thoughtful as she drove home from Maisey's. As it had turned out, Richard's grandmother hadn't asked for any explanations about his absence from the breakfast table and Anna Louise hadn't offered any. Now that she thought about it, Maisey had actually seemed downright upbeat when she'd discovered that her grandson had taken off. Maybe she'd figured her scheming was paying off, if it had Richard on the run.

Fortunately, Anna Louise didn't have a lot of time to worry about it. Luke Hall's oldest boy, Jeremy, and his girlfriend were coming in to talk about wedding plans. It was going to take every last bit of Anna Louise's persuasive skills to convince them they were too young to even consider getting married.

As she drove up to the church, she found Jeremy already pacing on the front lawn. Tall and gangly, his blond hair slicked back, he'd done his best to look grown-up in nice, navy blue pants, a dress shirt and a tie. It must have been an old shirt because the collar seemed strained around his neck and the too short sleeves revealed his bony wrists. Still, she complimented him.

"You look very handsome, Jeremy. Where's Maribeth?"

"She should be here in just a minute. Her ma made her baby-sit this morning and she was running late getting back."

"Well, I'm glad we have a few minutes alone. Come on inside and let's talk." She led the way into her office, which had its own entrance at the side of the parsonage. She pulled an extra chair around from behind her desk and sat down. Jeremy remained awkwardly standing.

"Sit down, Jeremy."

"I'm just a mite nervous, Pastor Perkins," he admitted. "It's not every day a man makes plans to get married."

"No, it's not," she agreed, then seized the chance to play up his apparent nervousness. "Are you sure this is something you're ready to do?"

Troubled eyes met her gaze. "Why, sure," he said, but his voice lacked conviction. "Me and Maribeth, we've been planning this ever since we were kids."

"And how old are you now?"

"I'm eighteen," he said, standing a little taller.

"And Maribeth?"

"She just turned seventeen, right after graduation. She's real smart. She skipped the third grade."

Anna Louise bit back a stern lecture about a girl of seventeen and a boy of eighteen being in no position to know their own minds, especially when all of their experiences had been limited to life in a tiny town like Kiley. From what she knew, both Jeremy and Maribeth were smarter than average. It would be a terrible waste for them to forgo the chance at a college education.

She hesitated long enough to consider her options. Maybe she could use Jeremy's own fears to get him to postpone the date for the wedding. If she came at him head-on, he'd fight her for sure. And going to Luke Hall or to Maribeth's parents would be no solution at all. He'd resent her interference and end up eloping.

"Do you have a job, Jeremy?"

"Sure. I work for my father at the store."

"I seem to recall that Maribeth used to talk about wanting to teach school. And weren't you interested in architecture or engineering at one time? You can't do either of those without a college education."

Her comments didn't seem to daunt him in the slightest. "We've thought about that, ma'am. I figure in a year or two we'll have some money saved and maybe we can move over to Charlottesville and go to school nights."

Anna Louise nodded. "That's possible, I suppose." She looked him squarely in the eye. "Unless Maribeth gets pregnant."

His eyes widened at that. "We're not planning on having kids right away," he said adamantly. "We've discussed it. We're going to be real careful. Maribeth's already..." He flushed with obvious embarrassment. "Well, she and the doc have talked about it. It's all taken care of."

Anna Louise was relieved on that count at least. "That's good. I'd hate to see your plans spoiled by a baby you hadn't expected. Of course, it seems to me that you could ensure that wouldn't happen if you'd both get into college first."

He blinked at her. "First? You mean, before we even get married?"

Jeremy sounded as if the idea had never once crossed his mind. "I know it would take real maturity to make a difficult decision like that," she admitted casually. "And you and Maribeth do love each other, but I was just thinking that a love you've shared since you were kids would surely last long enough to allow you both time to get your educations."

"But we..." He stumbled over whatever he'd been about to say. He regarded Anna Louise helplessly, then visibly gathered his courage. "What about sex?" he finally said bluntly. "It's not like we can go on waiting forever. I mean, it's really hard doing the right thing and staying clear of her until the wedding. Maybe you can't understand about that, not being married and all and being a preacher, but sometimes I think I'm just going to bust apart if I can't make love to her."

Anna Louise thought she had at least some idea what he meant. She'd been entertaining a few such notions herself since meeting Richard Walton, but she couldn't exactly share that with this eighteen-year-old boy.

"Jeremy, making love is something very beautiful to be shared by two people who have made a commitment to be together for the rest of their lives. I know waiting until you're married has been difficult. I'm proud of you for doing that." She regarded him intently. "But rushing into a marriage at eighteen, just so you can have sex, is wrong."

"Well, that's not the only reason we'd be getting married," he replied indignantly. "We love each other."

"But have you considered how much you'd be giving up by not waiting? You won't be able to afford a nice home for Maribeth on what you earn at your father's store."

His face fell. "Actually, we were going to have to live with my folks," he admitted.

"And what about taking your new wife out to a nice dinner once in a while? Or to a movie? Will there be money for that, if you're both trying to save for college? And what will Maribeth do for a job?"

"Mrs. Rawlings said she could use some extra help sewing."

Anna Louise could just imagine what Millicent Rawlings would pay. If it was even as much as minimum wage, she'd be surprised. "And how long would Maribeth be content doing that? She's a smart girl. You've said so yourself. How would you feel a year or two from now, if things didn't work out for college, after all? Wouldn't you be afraid she'd start resenting you because she missed that opportunity? Or that you might even resent her because you're stuck in the same old job at the general store right here in Kiley?''

Jeremy's expression turned bleak. "You don't think we should get married, do you?''

Hallelujah! Anna Louise thought, but she tried not to let her delight show. The battle wasn't won yet. He'd seen her point, but he hadn't agreed with her.

"It's not my decision, Jeremy. It's up to you and Maribeth. If her parents give her their permission to get married at seventeen and you want to go ahead with it, I'll conduct the ceremony and give you both my blessing.''

"But you think we're wrong," he persisted.

"I'm just not sure you've given it careful enough thought. When you have, I know you'll make the right decision.''

He regarded her worriedly. "How am I going to tell Maribeth what you've said? She's been counting on us getting married.''

"Don't tell her this is coming from me. Just talk to her the way I've been talking to you. Discuss all the ramifications. Maybe she'll realize all on her own that it's too soon.''

He sighed heavily and made his way to the door. "If we decide to go ahead, you won't fight us, will you?''

"No, Jeremy, I won't fight you. I only want what's best for both of you.''

"Thanks," he said, looking anything but grateful. In fact, he looked downright miserable. "I guess we'll be in touch."

"Take care. Tell Maribeth to stop by anytime if she wants to talk."

She watched Jeremy walk off toward town, his shoulders slumped. Maribeth Simmons, her pretty blond hair cascading down around her shoulders, met him on the road. He slid an arm around her waist and kissed the tip of her nose. Maribeth cast a troubled look back toward the parsonage, then walked on with her boyfriend.

Anna Louise sighed as they disappeared from sight. She thought she had gotten through to Jeremy, but there was no telling with kids that age. In the long run, if it came down to it, she'd rather see them married now than have to perform a shotgun wedding six months down the road. Thinking back to the confusion and uncertainties of that age, she realized she wouldn't want to be their age again for anything.

"You got something against marriage?"

Richard's voice from the doorway startled her. She hadn't heard the car drive up, so he must have walked down the hill. "Eavesdropping?" she asked, moving across the office to put the huge old oak desk safely between her and him.

"I didn't realize you had someone in here when I walked up to the door. As soon as I heard voices, I backed off to wait."

"Under a window, no doubt."

He shrugged. "Force of habit. That's how I get some of my best information."

"By sneaking around?"

"I prefer to think of it as clever, investigative reporting tactics."

"Call it what you will, it's still not right," she said, not one bit sure why she was making such an issue of it. The conversation had been private, but it had hardly contained significant secrets. In fact, if she had to guess, she'd say half the town would know what she and Jeremy had discussed before suppertime. He and Maribeth would tell their best friends, who'd tell their friends, who'd be overheard by their parents.

"I didn't come down here so you could catalog my sins or make judgments about my professional ethics," Richard informed her, drawing her attention away from how quickly gossip spread in Kiley.

"Why did you come?"

"Why else? Maisey had an idea."

Anna Louise had to laugh at the resigned expression on his face. "I'm surprised she sent you to do her bidding or that you agreed to come."

"We're having an Indian summer heat wave. It's eighty-eight degrees out there and she threatened to walk down here herself, if I didn't come."

"You might have suggested she call."

"I did. She had the idea you wouldn't agree unless one of us was here in person to persuade you."

Anna Louise regarded him suspiciously. "Persuade me to do what?"

"She thought maybe you'd like to come by later for a dip in Willow Creek and a picnic. It could be the last chance before cold weather comes."

The thought of a relaxing, cool swim tempted her just as Maisey had known it would. She'd been swimming in the creek almost every afternoon before Richard had come home. Since his arrival, she'd been uncomfortable with the idea and had stayed away. The thought of his experienced, womanizing eyes assessing her body when she was clad in nothing more than a bathing suit, no matter how unrevealing, had disconcerted her. It still did, especially since she could see he was viewing the prospect with some interest.

"I'd better not," she said. "I have a busy day."

"Too busy to take time for dinner?"

"Will you be there?" she inquired bluntly.

He grinned at that. "Oh, yes, I am definitely part of the package. Maisey saw to that right off. She's making Virginia ham sandwiches on homemade biscuits and potato salad, two of my favorite things."

Anna Louise's mouth watered. Maisey's potato salad was the best she'd ever had, with its bits of bacon, celery seed and a touch of mustard.

"Tempted?" he asked.

"Yes," she said without thinking, then added hurriedly, "no."

"Which is it?"

"I'm tempted, but I'm turning you down. Tell Maisey I'm sorry."

He looked troubled by her refusal. "Anna Louise, don't stay away on my account. There's no reason to."

"Oh, yes, there is," she said softly, letting him interpret that however he liked. "Now if you'll excuse me, I have work to do."

To her relief, he didn't argue. At the door, he paused. "If you change your mind, we'll be at the creek about five. That'll give us a bit of time before the sun sets."

"I won't change my mind," she said firmly.

"We'll see," he said in that smug way that set her teeth on edge.

She didn't watch him leave, didn't even permit herself to think about him for the next few hours as she caught up on paperwork. It was four o'clock when she finally yawned and stretched, then put down her pen and shoved aside the calculator she'd been using to balance the accounts. They were still several hundred dollars short of the amount needed for a new roof. For the life of her she couldn't think of how they were going to raise it. Everybody in town was stretched to the limit. Kiley, never particularly prosperous, had been hard hit by the recession.

Well, she reminded herself sternly, the Lord had a way of providing. She'd just have to have faith that an inspiration would come to her.

Walking through the doorway that connected the office to her private quarters, she paused by the answering machine, startled by the sight of a blinking light. Almost everyone in town knew they could reach her at the church office during the day. Why would anyone have left a message on her personal machine?

The first thought that crossed her mind was that something had happened to one of her parents. But she dismissed that almost as quickly as it occurred to her. They would have called the office, as well.

The obvious way to find out was to punch the play button, but she did it with some reluctance. Her unvoiced fears were validated when she heard the first condemning words of the message.

"You're defiling the church of Kiley," the strained voice began. "Unless you give up and go back where you belong, you will be damned forever and the people of Kiley along with you." The man added several passages of Scripture to support his claim, all in a righteous tone.

Anna Louise listened to the rambling diatribe all the way through to the end, then sighed wearily. The caller hadn't said anything she hadn't heard a hundred times before. From her own pastor in Tennessee to her colleagues at seminary, just about everyone had told her she was wrong to insist on becoming a preacher. They didn't understand that the calling had been every bit as powerful for her as it had been for them. Or if they did understand that much, they thought she should have been satisfied with a more traditional role.

"Teach Sunday school," one friend had suggested.

"Graduate from seminary, if you must, but just take a chaplaincy in a hospital. Folks are used to being cared for by women there. They won't blink an eye if you come to pray with them. Just don't force yourself into a job that God never meant to be held by a woman."

She'd countered that one by reeling off passages of Scripture of her own. Unfortunately she couldn't fight an anonymous caller who left messages and never confronted her face-to-face. Listening to the all-too-familiar criticism didn't frighten her nearly so much as it exhausted her. She wondered if there would come a day when she would no longer have the strength to fight those who opposed her, people who shared Pastor Orville Patterson's beliefs.

She doubted that had been Orville on the phone. He didn't waste time with anonymous harassment. He was vocal and obvious about his objections. She doubted there was a soul in the entire Shenandoah Valley who didn't know where Orville stood on the subject of her being pastor of the Kiley church and his five-year fight to have her removed. Up until now, though, he hadn't had the votes. Those two new pastors had seemingly changed the balance of power.

Erasing the message, she drew in a deep breath and made up her mind to go to Willow Creek, after all. Somehow the prospect of spending a night alone in this house, perhaps getting even more threatening calls, was more than she could bear.

Upstairs, she put on her swimsuit under a pair of knee-length shorts and a shapeless blouse that she knotted at the waist. Only at the last second as she drove up the hill did she wonder if she wasn't leaving the frying pan to jump straight into the fire.

Richard spread a blanket on the bank alongside Willow Creek where it curved behind Maisey's property and formed a cool, shimmering pond. He moved the heavy picnic basket to the middle of the blanket. When he looked up, he spotted Maisey making her way along the bank, lugging a folding chair. He rushed to take it from her.

"I told you I'd come back to get the chair," he scolded.

"It doesn't weigh much more than a feather," she argued. "Besides, I feel better when I'm being useful."

"Wasn't fixing this picnic useful enough? That basket weighs a ton. What's in there, anyway? Did you make a batch of biscuits that turned out like bricks?"

"Very funny. You know my biscuits always turn out light and fluffy."

"Then how many ham-and-biscuit sandwiches did you put in there? Enough for the whole town?"

"I know how you eat, young man, especially after you've put in a hard day's work. You've been tussling with the wallpaper for the parlor all day. And Anna Louise can usually be persuaded to eat several."

"I told you she wasn't coming," he reminded her.

"We'll see," she said, just as he had to Anna Louise earlier.

He'd had time to think about it since then and had decided that he'd been overly confident about her having a change of heart. "Do you want to wade a bit now or are you hungry?" he asked Maisey.

"You go for your swim. I think I'll sit right here in the shade and rest a bit."

Richard was in the middle of the creek, enjoying the way the refreshingly cool water slid over his bare skin when he heard Anna Louise's voice.

"Well, I'll be damned," he muttered, his gaze fixed on her as she sashayed into view. He kept his eyes on her as she chatted with Maisey, then slowly stripped off her shorts and blouse to reveal a black, one-piece bathing suit that she obviously thought was sedate.

Somebody ought to explain to her that she was still baring enough skin to make a man's heart thunder in his chest. And what was covered wasn't exactly a mystery. That suit molded itself to her in a way that revealed every tantalizing curve, from her generous bosom to her nipped-in waist and her rounded bottom. He dove beneath the surface of the creek in the misguided hope that the water would cool his suddenly overheated libido.

It didn't work. When he surfaced, he was surprised to see that there wasn't any steam rising from the spot where his hot skin came into contact with the cool water.

A ripple in the surface of the water warned him barely an instant before Anna Louise swam into view beside him with long, clean strokes that cut smoothly through the water.

"I'm surprised to see you," he said as she stood up and brushed the strands of red hair back from a face that was so breathtakingly perfect it almost brought his heart skidding to a halt. He studied each feature, lingering at her full, tempting lips, before finally settling his gaze on her eyes. That's when he detected the faint hint of dismay. He had a gut feeling that it wasn't his blatant survey that was troubling her.

"Are you okay?"

"Sure," she said blithely. Too blithely.

"What's going on, Anna Louise? Something's wrong. I can see it in your eyes."

She shook her head, spraying him with droplets of water that dried almost instantly on his heated flesh. "Nothing I can't handle."

He was troubled by the sense that she was all bravado. "Would you ask for help if you needed it?"

"I'm not a fool," she said stiffly. "Of course, I would."

He gave a curt nod of satisfaction. That would have to do for now. He forced a challenging note into his voice. "Race you to the willow tree at the curve."

Her expression relaxed at once and laughter danced in her eyes. "You're on."

Richard had expected to win easily, but she matched him stroke for stroke. When they were within a few feet of the finishing mark and he was in danger of being beaten or at least tied, he deliberately swam into her path. The slight brush had her sputtering with indignation as their legs tangled and they both went under.

"You lousy, rotten cheat," she said to him when she could catch her breath.

"It was an accident," he swore.

"Right."

"I saw that, Richard Walton," Maisey called from the shore. "You deliberately bumped into Anna Louise to keep her from beating you."

"Did not," he said, but he couldn't help laughing at the sight of both women standing up to him with such fierce determination over a silly race. He turned back to Anna Louise. "I'll race you to the blanket. Loser fixes a plate for the winner."

"A fair race?" she countered.

"Cross my heart," he said, making the gesture.

While he was trying to reassure her, the sweet pastor of Kiley's oldest church splashed a handful of water into his eyes and took off for the bank of the creek. He was still blinking when he looked around and found her standing triumphantly in the middle of the blanket.

"Don't forget to put mustard on my sandwiches," she called out cheerfully.

He climbed out of the creek and tried to keep a menacing glare in his eyes as he approached her. "You'll be lucky if I don't cram them down your throat," he warned.

She laughed at him. "You're all talk, Richard Walton."

"I must say I have to agree with her," Maisey said, clearly egging Anna Louise on.

He scowled at his grandmother. *"Et tu, Brute?"*

Clearly unintimidated by the accusation, Maisey sat back and smoothed her skirt over her knees. "I believe I'm ready for dinner now," she informed him primly.

"Me, too," Anna Louise chimed in.

"Then, by all means, let me serve you." He dished up the potato salad, added the ham and biscuits and fresh tomato slices, then passed the first plate over to Maisey. When he gave Anna Louise hers, he leaned close to her ear and whispered, "I will get even with you, Pastor Perkins."

Her brown eyes widened at the teasing threat in his voice. She swallowed hard, but her gaze remained unblinking. "I guess that means I'll have to stay on my toes, then, doesn't it?"

He grinned. "You bet."

The conversation shifted then to easy, uncontroversial topics. Maisey drifted to sleep after a while, leaving Richard and Anna Louise talking softly about childhood memories.

"I recall the time I wrote an essay about wanting to be a preacher," she divulged. "I must have been about ten. We'd been asked to describe what we wanted to be when we grew up. I was so proud of that essay. My parents had read it and thought it was wonderful."

"Did you get an A?"

He could see the shake of her head in the gathering twilight. "I failed."

He regarded her with a sense of shock. "Why?"

"The teacher tore it up. She said I had no business writing such blasphemous things. The way she said it, I felt as if I'd done something terrible, as if I'd written that I wanted to be a murderer or something."

"What did your parents do?"

"When I told them, they explained to me that if I was serious about becoming a pastor, then I had to learn to deal with people like that teacher. I think that was the day I grew up. I know it was the day I resolved never to let what other people think rule my decisions."

"And you never wavered from your dream?"

"Never once," she said quietly. "Never once."

Richard recalled how fervently he had believed in his own dream of traveling the world, reporting on things that needed changing, making a difference.

Proving himself, he realized suddenly, just as Anna Louise meant to do. In that moment of self-discovery, he saw that there was at least one thing he and Anna Louise had in common. They both fought tooth and nail for what they believed in, against what some would see as insurmountable odds.

Silence fell around them then, but it was the compatible silence born of budding friendship and understanding. For just about the first time since he'd met Anna Louise, he felt totally comfortable. As always, he was sharply aware of her as a woman, but he was even more aware of her as a person of strength and character, a person deserving of admiration.

The pleasant mood was disrupted only minutes later by the splatter of the first fat drops of rain.

"You get Maisey up to the house," Anna Louise said, her face turned up to the rain as if she were a flower in need of healing moisture. "I'll bring the picnic things."

Richard nodded. He woke Maisey, helped her up, and with an arm around her waist, led her back to the house. He was on his way back to the creek when he saw Anna Louise coming. She wasn't rushing. If anything, she looked as if she was enjoying every drop of the cleansing shower. Richard took the picnic basket from her.

"Don't you want to come in and dry off?" he said when she immediately turned toward her car.

"No. I'd just get wet all over again when I do leave. I believe I'll be going on home."

For the first time in as far back as he could remember, Richard suddenly felt tongue-tied. "I'm glad you decided to come tonight."

She turned slowly back at that. Her gaze rose and clashed with his. "Me, too," she said softly. "I feel more peaceful now."

As she walked away, Richard was left to wonder exactly what she had meant. Peaceful? Not him. He felt as if he'd been poleaxed from a direction in which he'd least expected it.

Chapter Seven

It was the sixth straight day of rain. It had started the night of Anna Louise's picnic with Maisey and Richard and hadn't let up for a minute since. Her spirits were almost as gloomy as the weather.

Worse than her own building depression, Willow Creek was rising, testing the limits of the soggy banks. Word from upstream was even more worrisome, with weather forecasters predicting another two or three days of pounding, soaking deluges.

Anna Louise walked through the shadowy aisles of the church, shifting the pitiful assortment of pots and pans to collect water from the worst of the leaks. She'd already spread plastic tarps over most of the pews, hoping to save the wood. The carved altar was shrouded in plastic, as well.

Anna Louise sighed at the mess. Another six months and they would have had the new roof. As it was, she'd be conducting Sunday services in an atmosphere as damp and uncomfortable as an open-air pavilion in the midst of a hurricane.

When she'd done what she could, she walked to the vestibule and looked out the front door. The creek appeared to be creeping up inch by inch even as she watched. Fortunately, most of the houses in Kiley were on higher land and weren't threatened by a flood. Only her church, sitting barely a hundred yards from the creek where the land leveled off, stood directly in the path of the rising water.

She had two choices and it was time to make one of them. She could call on God to stop the rain or call on her parishioners to divert the flooding waters. Since she never liked to push too hard in asking God to alter His plans, she headed for the phone in her office to call on her human resources. But just in case He wasn't entirely set in His ways this time, she did murmur a fervent request toward Heaven while she was at it.

An hour later the rain hadn't let up, but there was a scene of organized chaos on the sloping front lawn of the church. More than a dozen men and women were filling bags with sand to shore up the creek banks. Luke Hall and his wife had closed down the store and come at once, bringing Jeremy and their other sons. Maribeth had followed Jeremy. Tucker Patterson, the Monroes, the Hensons and even old Millicent Rawlings were doing what they could.

But as hard as everyone was working, Anna Louise recognized that their energy and know-how were pitifully inadequate. The water was already up to Anna Louise's ankles and she was a good three yards from what had been the creek bank until just a little while ago.

"You'll never save the church at this rate," Richard observed, voicing Anna Louise's own fears.

She hadn't seen him arrive, but she should have known word of the struggle to save the church would reach Maisey. And whatever Richard's personal beliefs were these days, he respected Maisey's. Anna Louise should have known he would come to help. She didn't want to consider too closely why she hadn't called and directly asked for his help herself. Maybe it had something to do with the longing she'd felt when she'd left Willow Creek after the picnic a few days earlier. She hadn't been able to shake the feeling that she was more attracted to Richard Walton than she had any business being.

At the moment, however, she found his know-it-all attitude irritating. She wiped a strand of wet hair from her eyes and scowled up at him.

"You could pitch in and help," she suggested pointedly.

"It's a losing battle, at least the way you're going about it."

Anna Louise lost patience. "Do you have a better idea? If not, get out of my way and let me get back to work." She shoved past him and sloshed through the rising water.

He stayed where he was and called after her, "Seems to me you'd be better off diverting the stream's path upstream, just below Maisey's where the land first begins to level off."

Anna Louise paused to listen.

"There are open fields to the south. If we send the water that way, then the church would be out of harm's way. Better yet, when the water's receded, that land should be more fertile than ever."

Anna Louise nodded agreeably. "Good idea. Too bad it won't work."

Hands on his hips, he glowered at her. "I wasn't aware you had experience with the Army Corps of Engineers," Richard retorted.

He was obviously miffed that she'd dismissed his idea so readily. She didn't have time to indulge his ego. "True," she shot right back. "My experience is with Orville Patterson. It's his land and he won't allow what you're suggesting, not if I ask anyway."

An expression of genuine bewilderment crept over his face. "Why the hell not?"

"Do you even have to ask?"

"Surely you're not suggesting that Orville would take out his feud with you on the church itself. He's not that small-minded."

"I thought you'd pinned that label on the whole town. Is Orville an exception just because he was once your childhood buddy? I can't say I've seen the two of you together even once since you've been back."

"You're right. We haven't even spoken. But this has nothing to do with me. Orville's a pastor himself, for goodness' sake. How could he justify letting the church be destroyed or even just damaged by flood waters if it was in his power to prevent it?''

"Let me share a few hard truths about your old friend Orville,'' Anna Louise retorted. "He doesn't just dislike me. He doesn't just quietly disapprove of my career. He feels he has a moral obligation to show me the error of my ways. He'll view this flood and any destruction it causes as a sign from God that he's right. He won't allow anyone to interfere, not even his own father, or you can be sure Tucker would have offered to talk to him.''

She gestured toward the small crew she'd been able to rally. "Take a look around. I called twice this many people, but these are the only ones who showed up. Orville got to the others. Naturally that's not what they told me. They all had high-sounding excuses, but I'd wager my last dollar that they were trumped up at the sound of my voice. If we try to flood Orville's land, we may lose some of these volunteers, too.''

Richard's jaw set in a way she was beginning to recognize.

"Then we won't say just what we're up to,'' he said flatly. "Come on. Let's get busy.''

As he took off upstream, calling to the others to follow, Anna Louise ran after him. "You can't do this,'' she shouted after him, trying to make him see reason. "It'll just make things worse.''

"It'll save the church, won't it?'' He gave her what seemed to pass for a smile with him. "Don't worry,

Anna Louise. I know some of Orville's most wretched childhood sins. He won't mess with me.''

Anna Louise stared after him as he stalked off. Somehow the thought that Richard was willing to resort to blackmail on her behalf wasn't much comfort. But that didn't keep her from following after him and pitching in. It helped to see that Tucker Patterson had gone along with the plan without an apparent qualm.

Another load of donated sand was dumped upstream. From noon until darkness fell they did what they could to divert the rising waters of Willow Creek and send them off on a new, less destructive path.

Anna Louise's shoulders ached. Her arms burned with a searing pain from the constant lifting. Her clothes were soaked through. Her hair clung to her head in a tangle of wet curls. She could barely put one foot in front of the other when Richard came to her and put his hands on her shoulders.

"Enough. Take the other women and go home. I'll stay here with the men and keep at it for as long as it takes. Luke's bringing some floodlights out.''

As tempted as she was by the thought of a hot shower, dry clothes and a warm fire, Anna Louise shook her head. "It's my responsibility.''

Hard blue eyes stared into hers. "And now it's mine.''

"Why would you do this for us?''

He shrugged. "Don't go nominating me for sainthood, Anna Louise. It's just something that needs doing.''

She gave him an exhausted smile. "Why do you fight so hard to convince everyone what a hard heart you have, Richard Walton?"

"Because that's the truth," he said evenly, his gaze never wavering. "Don't forget it, Pastor Perkins."

He turned then and walked away. Anna Louise stood staring after him, her own heart aching. If he couldn't see the goodness in other people quite yet, why couldn't he at least admit to the goodness inside himself? "You're a kind, decent man, Richard Walton," she murmured. "Someday I'm going to get you to recognize that."

Banished from further sandbagging by that very same kind, decent man, she rounded up the other women. "The men are going to keep at this for a few more hours. Let's go make them some hot coffee, soup and sandwiches. They'll need them when they're through."

Luke Hall's wife volunteered to raid the general store for cheese and cold cuts. Nate Dorsey's wife, Kathryn, offered to gather the last of the fresh vegetables from her garden for the soup. Patty Sue Henson had some beef stock she'd frozen. She donated that to go with the vegetables. Maribeth Simmons gave Anna Louise a shy smile and offered to run home for loaves of fresh-baked bread her mother had made that morning. Tucker Patterson overheard their plans and volunteered to go by the drugstore and pick up all the thermos bottles he had in stock so they could bring the coffee and soup out to the men.

By the time the other women returned, Anna Louise had started the huge coffee urn they used for church suppers. She and Kathryn Dorsey got to work chopping the fresh onions, green beans, carrots and potatoes, while the beef stock defrosted and began to simmer on the oversize stove in the parsonage's restaurant-style kitchen. The house itself might be tiny, but the original founders of the church had seen the need for a kitchen that could prepare meals for the entire congregation. Rather than putting it in a church hall they couldn't afford to build, anyway, they'd just put it in the pastor's residence, which had turned the house into the center of church activities. Anna Louise, who loved to entertain, had always liked it that way.

Tonight, filled with the aroma of beef stew simmering on the stove and fresh coffee perking, the house felt cozy despite the steady pounding of the rain on the old-fashioned tin roof. The atmosphere had been so congenial with everyone working side by side that she felt for a moment as if the threatening flood had been something of a blessing. The sense of community often sparked by crises was one of the things she liked best about life in a small town.

She was thinking about that and stirring a second pot of stew, while the other women carried the first round out to the men, when she sensed that she was no longer alone. She glanced over her shoulder and saw Richard standing in the middle of the kitchen, looking like a drowned cat. His heavy-duty yellow slicker had long since been shed because of the unseasonal

October heat and his hair looked as if he'd just stepped from a shower. He looked disheveled in a way that was astonishingly sexy.

"Good heavens, you're soaked clear through," she said. She sounded flustered, possibly because of the tantalizing way his shirt was clinging to his broad shoulders and the even more intriguing way his pants molded to his narrow hips and lean legs. "Since the sun's gone down, it's getting cold out there. I'll get you some towels so you can dry off."

"Don't bother, unless you mind me dripping on the linoleum. I'll need to get back outside in a minute, anyway."

"Don't worry about the floor. I'll have another batch of stew ready shortly. Sit down and I'll bring you a cup of coffee while you wait."

"I can get the coffee." His gaze met hers. "You okay?"

"Of course. Why would you ask?"

"You seem nervous."

Anna Louise shook her head, denying the effect he had on her as much for her own benefit as his. "Not nervous, just harried. How's it going out there?"

"It's too soon to say for sure, but it looks as if the water's going where we've diverted it. As long as the creek doesn't rise too high and the sandbags hold, we should be okay."

"Any sign of Orville?"

He grinned. "He did pass by about an hour ago."

"Oh, dear. What did he have to say?"

"Plenty, as a matter of fact."

Anna Louise groaned. "I knew it. This is only going to make matters worse."

Richard shook his head. "I don't think so. Before he could get too carried away with his hand-of-God tirade, I pointed out how it would look for a pastor not to do everything in his power to save a church. Told him the incident just might be viewed as important enough to be picked up and carried on the national wire services. He settled right down. Even pitched in and hauled a few sandbags."

Anna Louise's mouth dropped open in astonishment. "He helped?"

"Long enough to make sure everyone saw him. By now, though, I suspect he's home by the fire feeling downright self-righteous."

"Well, I'll be." She regarded him sternly. "Not that I approve of blackmailing the man to get your way."

"It's hardly blackmail, Anna Louise. I just pointed out how his actions might be viewed by those cynical members of the press."

"And considering your expertise in that area, he had to take you seriously."

"I'm sure it helped," he conceded with a spark of pure mischief in his eyes. He didn't look one whit troubled by his deviousness. "Of course, Orville is a pragmatic man. Once he'd thought about the implications, the decision became clear enough."

"I suppose." She turned to face him. "I really don't know how I'm ever going to thank you for helping today."

"I'm not doing any more than anyone else out there. Young Jeremy seems to have a knack for engineering. He had a plan sketched out by the time we got to Orville's property. It was a damn good one, too. He mentioned the conversation you had with him the other day about getting his college degree before getting married. I didn't tell him I'd overheard most of it."

"I hope you backed me up."

"I didn't need to. He confided to me that Maribeth agreed to wait. They'll both be going to college starting in January, after they've saved enough for the first semester. Apparently she'd been offered a partial scholarship, but she'd been afraid to tell him about it because she didn't want to disappoint him."

"She was prepared to go through with the wedding just to please him?" Anna Louise shook her head. "That just proves they're too young."

"I don't know. It sounded like the unselfish act of a woman in love to me."

Anna Louise scowled at the overly romantic notion. "I'm just glad they took the time to talk things through before they both ruined their lives."

"Just one thing," Richard said.

"What's that?"

"I doubt you're going to keep the two of them pure and innocent through four years of college."

"Who knows?" she said with confidence. "Miracles do happen."

"I'm not sure miracles are any match for rampant teenage hormones."

"If Jeremy and Maribeth were mature enough to make this decision about postponing their wedding and going to college, then I think they can be trusted to do the right thing when it comes to sex."

"Are we talking about your idea of the right thing or theirs?"

Anna Louise frowned at the suggestion that there could be two different interpretations of right. Values were values. "I'm not here to impose my will on anybody," she shot back irritably. "I try to teach values and faith, but one thing we were all given as a birthright is free will. We all have to make our own decisions about how to apply the teachings of the church."

"Sounds like pretty liberal thinking to me. Does that mean that a jaded journalist could steal a kiss from the town preacher without setting off a hail of fire and brimstone?"

Anna Louise's breath seemed to be lodged somewhere in her throat. The question seemed to have come from out of the blue. A few nights ago, in the intimacy of darkness beside Willow Creek, it wouldn't have surprised her so. Now they were both bedraggled and exhausted. It was an astonishing time to think of seduction.

Her gaze narrowed suspiciously. "Why would you want to?"

"The usual reasons, I suppose." His gaze clashed with hers. "And because at this moment, standing there all flushed and mussed up, you are the most attractive woman I have ever seen and you surely do look as if you could use a kiss." As if he sensed her need to be persuaded, he added, "Nothing too improper, of course. Just something to warm us both before we get back to the damp business of saving the church."

Her heart began to thump unsteadily. Suddenly she was craving the most improper kiss imaginable. This wasn't good. It wasn't good at all.

Still, she lifted her chin until she could look Richard directly in the eyes. "I suppose it's my duty to send you back to work with a little something to warm you," she said primly. When he moved closer, his expression hopeful, she stood on tiptoe and gave him a very proper peck on the cheek.

Laughter lit his eyes. "Oh, Anna Louise, that kiss was downright pitiful. It wouldn't warm toast." He bent his head down until his mouth hovered above hers. Their breath mingled for a heartbeat and then his lips touched hers.

Anna Louise thought it was entirely possible she was going to faint. Richard's kiss was indeed a definite improvement over her own pathetic attempt. It was a warm, coaxing kiss with just enough impure intent behind it to send her pulse skittering wildly.

Just when Anna Louise was considering abandoning any pretense at restraint, she heard a sudden indrawn breath. Jerking away from Richard's loose embrace, she turned to look directly into Maribeth Simmons's shocked face.

The teenager had flushed red with embarrassment. "I'm sorry," she muttered. "I didn't know...I didn't realize that... Oh, dear."

Richard didn't appear the least bit nonplussed at being caught in a compromising position. Of course, given his worldly reputation, one kiss wouldn't do a thing to hurt his image. In fact, there was talk around town of far worse exploits back in his high school days. She'd heard of more blatant incidents of rebelliousness than the theft of Mabel Hartley's girdle. Folks probably wouldn't bat an eye over this, at least where he was concerned.

Anna Louise, however, was mortified.

Oblivious to Anna Louise's dismay, or determined to put the best possible face on things because of it—Anna Louise couldn't be sure which—Richard winked at Maribeth. He looked downright unrepentant.

"Pastor Perkins was feeling a little down in the dumps about the weather. I was just trying to boost her spirits a little. You know how it is," he said cheerfully.

"Sure, I suppose," Maribeth replied, still a little wide-eyed with shock.

Richard gave the teenager a quick kiss on the cheek, as if to emphasize that his kissing Anna Louise had been no more serious in intent. "See you two."

When he had gone and Anna Louise could manage to speak, she said, "Maribeth, I hope you didn't misinterpret what you saw."

"I don't think so." Suddenly she grinned at Anna Louise. "It looks to me like Mr. Walton has a serious crush on you."

"Nonsense," Anna Louise said quickly. "He was just...just...well, you heard him. He was trying to cheer me up."

"Jeremy tries to cheer me up a lot, too. It works, doesn't it?" she inquired, her expression thoroughly innocent.

Anna Louise finally gave up. "As a matter of fact," she admitted, "it was very effective."

Richard didn't see a sign of Anna Louise for the next two weeks. She didn't set foot on Walton property or, if she did, she came when he wasn't around. He knew what was keeping her away. She was troubled by that kiss. He had felt her response as she had curled into his body. He had been aware of her sweet surrender.

And, to be perfectly honest, what had begun as a game had ended up scaring the dickens out of him, as well. He had liked the way her body fit so perfectly against his. He had been surprised by the way his blood had pulsed harder and hotter just from the touch of her mouth against his.

Anna Louise, it seemed, was likely to continue to astonish him.

He admired the way she had pitched in to shore up the banks of the creek. He was even more admiring when he heard from neighbors that she'd once sat up half the night with cantankerous old Mr. Jordan, when moonshine had given him the blues, which it had on a regular basis every Friday night for the past fifty years. Day after day there were new examples of her generosity and caring.

To his deep regret, Richard found himself longing for more of her warmth and attention. That purely masculine yearning made him grateful that she was steering as far away from him as she could. He didn't trust his own willpower any more to cause him to do the right thing.

Fortunately, even Maisey seemed to have pulled back in her attempts to throw them together. He didn't doubt that it was a temporary slowdown, but he was grateful for whatever time he could get to gather his thoughts and shore up those barriers he'd erected around his heart long ago.

He worked long, hot hours in the orchard, tiring himself out thoroughly so that he fell into bed each night exhausted. He didn't want to think about Anna Louise Perkins for even an instant. He didn't want to feel the sensations she'd aroused in him.

For the most part, the plan worked. The only thing he couldn't seem to control were his dreams, and Anna Louise, darn her sexy little hide, turned up in more and more of them.

Chapter Eight

Anna Louise hadn't been able to look Maribeth Simmons in the eye since that night in her kitchen when the teenage girl had caught her being kissed by Richard. In fact, if she hadn't had duties at the church to attend to, she might very well have taken to her bed, pulled the covers over her head and stayed there until Maribeth left for college at the start of the second semester.

As it was, Anna Louise was certainly getting a lot of paperwork done. In her determination to avoid another confusing encounter with Richard, she spent every spare minute locked away in her office. When Maisey called to ask what was keeping her away, she said she had a special project for the church council that had to be completed.

It wasn't exactly a lie. She had been assigned to make a report at the next meeting of the pastors from all of the neighboring counties, but she had finished it weeks ago. If she typed it over a hundred times, it wouldn't take up all the time she'd claimed to need for it.

"You're working too hard, dear," Maisey said worriedly. "You looked a mite peaked at services on Sunday."

"I haven't been getting much sleep," she admitted with some caution. The last thing she wanted was to alarm Maisey or to put any notions into her head about why she might suddenly be unable to fall asleep the minute her head touched the pillow.

"Perhaps you should see Doc Benson for a tonic."

"No. I'm just a little restless. I'm sure it will pass. It probably has something to do with the change of seasons. Have you noticed that just about all the leaves have turned? We're truly into autumn now. It'll be Thanksgiving before we know it and then Christmas."

Maisey made a sound that might have been agreement or a barely muffled chuckle. Anna Louise preferred to think it was the former. That was the only reason she dared to mention the man who'd put her in such a state. "I haven't seen Richard around town the last few days," she said casually.

Maisey, blast her, chuckled out loud this time. "I wondered if that might be what's troubling you."

"Troubling me," she said indignantly. "Of course not. I was just wondering if he'd taken sick after helping to fight the flood. I feel responsible for involving him in all that."

"It was his decision, Anna Louise. You should know him well enough by now to realize that he never does anything that doesn't suit him. Anyway, you have nothing to worry about. It would take more than a few hours of hard labor to tire him out."

Her breath caught in her throat. "He hasn't left, has he? I know how much you wanted him to stay through the holidays at least."

If Maisey felt like laughing at the blatant probing, she displayed admirable restraint. Her voice was perfectly even when she said, "He hasn't left, not for good, anyway. He went to Washington for a couple of days to talk to his editor at the paper."

The explanation wasn't as reassuring as it might have been. Anna Louise's heart seemed to skid to a halt. "Is he there to discuss his next assignment?"

"He didn't really say. I suppose that could be it. To be honest, he hasn't seemed all that anxious to leave lately. I wonder why that is?" she taunted.

Anna Louise didn't care to offer her personal interpretation of Richard's actions. It was probably just wishful thinking on her part, anyway. "I'm sure I don't know," she said stiffly. "You must be glad that he's not about to run off again, though."

"Oh, I expect I'm not the only one," Maisey said dryly. "Quite a few people seem to have taken to him. He's been getting several calls from Penelope King. They used to date in high school, you know. She's been living over in Jasper Junction since her divorce.

She found out from Orville that Richard was back and the phone hasn't stopped ringing since.''

"Do you suppose that's why he's staying on?" Anna Louise asked, trying not to allow any hint of jealousy or dismay to creep into her voice. Given Maisey's sharp ears, she doubted she was successful. Besides, Maisey had obviously made the comment in the first place just to taunt Anna Louise.

"He hasn't seen her yet, so far as I know. Of course, if I had to make a guess, I'd say he's beginning to feel at home here again. After what he's been through, a visit to Kiley was just what he needed."

"But he won't be satisfied around here for long," Anna Louise said, sounding defeated. "We must seem pretty dull compared to the life he usually leads."

"Oh, I don't know about that. Seems to me there's plenty to do around here. It's just a matter of having somebody point it out."

When Anna Louise got off the phone, she thought about what it would mean to Maisey to have Richard stay on in Kiley. She purposely did not examine what it might mean to her. If she'd stopped to consider the danger to her heart, she would have done anything in her power to get him to go, not stay.

"If it's a matter of keeping the man busy, then I can certainly do that," she said out loud with an air of grim determination. "Richard Walton won't have a spare minute from now until next summer if I have anything to say about it."

* * *

During his two days in Washington, Richard had had a lot of time to think about his decision to continue his leave of absence from the paper through the holidays. His boss was frankly astounded that he hadn't already freaked out from total boredom.

"I can't hold this position for you forever," foreign news editor Jim Curran had told him.

"Who are you kidding? The powers that be will probably be delighted to have me off the payroll for a few more months. They'll be able to save a few bucks."

"But if that slot stays empty long enough, they just might decide they can get along without you or anybody else filling it," he said, pointing out one of the hard realities about the journalism business. Even the best papers and networks were tightening up, cutting staff. "You're putting me in a helluva spot. I can't afford to be losing positions. It'll jeopardize our ability to provide decent coverage from overseas. Besides, you're the best man I have. I want you on the front lines, not wasting your talent in some hick town."

The flattery had missed its mark. "I know how good I am," Richard had told him without so much as a hint of humility. "And the best things in life are worth waiting for. I believe I read that somewhere."

Jim Curran regarded him grumpily. "Damn, you aren't sitting over there in the mountains turning philosophical on me, are you? I don't want you back if you're going to be turning in political essays, instead of hard news."

"Not a chance," he'd retorted, but in retrospect he wasn't so sure about that.

Anna Louise had him thinking about a lot of things in a different way. Mostly she had him thinking about her, about the way her hair glistened like fire in the sunlight, about her strength of purpose, about the way her lips had molded themselves to his, about her old-fashioned scent that reminded him of a summer garden. Damn, the woman was beginning to get under his skin. And to be perfectly truthful, she even had him wondering whether he wanted to go back overseas again. He didn't dare mention that to his boss. Not yet, anyway.

What amazed him the most, especially after some of the other opinionated, strong-willed women he'd known, was that Anna Louise knew when to be quiet. She had a way of letting the silence steal over them and work its magic. He'd discovered there was a certain comfort to be found in that.

Unfortunately, he realized when he returned to Kiley, Anna Louise also knew when to badger. He couldn't imagine what had come over her in the little bit of time he'd been gone. Obviously she'd gotten the wrong idea when he'd turned up to help save the church. In the misguided belief that he cared about the town, it looked as if she was going to get on his case every time there was a task that needed doing. This time it had something to do with a recreation hall she wanted built. Heavenly days, he thought with some regret, when Anna Louise got a bee in her bonnet, she didn't know when to quit.

"If everyone pitches in, we can have it built before the first snowfall," she told him enthusiastically. "It'll give the kids a place to go during the winter months. Just think, we'll be able to hold dances there. Maybe bingo games for the older folks. Why, I can't think of a single thing that would mean more to the town of Kiley. A few days, Richard. That's all it would take. Just like an old-fashioned barn raising."

That soft cajoling note in her voice was almost his undoing. But he steeled himself against it. "No way," he said, refusing to so much as look at her from his perch atop a ladder in his bedroom. Of all the rooms for Anna Louise to be in, this was the worst. He'd never be able to sleep again without envisioning her here.

Unfortunately, being at the top of a ladder, tangled in wallpaper with a nagging woman down below, put a man in the awkward position of saying yes to her demands or finding himself flat on the floor. Her hands seemed to be tightening their grip on the ladder in an ominous way. Still, he did try to wriggle off her hook.

"Go away, Anna Louise. Now's not the time for this," he called down stubbornly.

Her chin jutted up just as stubbornly. The ladder trembled just the teensiest bit. "The town needs this, Richard. All the other men have committed to helping."

"Is that supposed to persuade me? I'm not like the other men in this town. Just because I helped to save the church from the flood, don't go getting any ideas.

I have no stake here, no kids, no personal commitment." He meant every word of what he said, but for some reason the declaration lacked his usual fire.

"Maisey's here," she reminded him quietly. She allowed that to sink in, then added, "They're thinking of naming this recreation hall after her."

Richard sucked in a breath to recover from the direct hit. "They may name it after Maisey? Why?"

"She put up the bulk of the money for the lumber. Luke Hall is over in Charlottesville right now making arrangements for it to be delivered."

Shock sent his senses reeling. He had to cling to the top of his dresser to keep from tumbling to the floor. "Where the hell..." he began, but his voice trailed off. He suddenly guessed where Maisey had gotten the extra money. He'd been sending it to her since the day he'd left town. He'd known the minute he'd returned and seen the general state of disrepair around the property that she hadn't spent one dime of it on herself.

Below him, Anna Louise gave a nod of satisfaction. "Exactly," she said as if she knew what conclusion he'd reached. "It was the money you gave her. She saved every penny."

"Why would she give it to build a recreation hall?"

"That's something you'll have to ask her. Will you help?"

He heaved a massive sigh of resignation. "You knew when you came over here that I would."

She nodded. "It's all a matter of knowing which buttons to push, isn't it?" she said smugly. "See you in the morning?"

"What time?"

"They're planning to start at sunup, just like an old-fashioned barn raising. Won't that be fun?"

Fun didn't begin to cover it, he thought dismally. "I'll be there."

"With bells on," she added cheerfully. "You know the expression, right?"

He glared down at her. "I know the damned expression. I'll be there. Let's just let it go at that."

Anna Louise apparently chose to ignore his irritability. She shot him a smile that could have melted an iceberg. "Thanks," she said as if he'd granted her a generous favor instead of grudgingly caving in to her sweetly spoken blackmail.

Before long she'd have him becoming a part of the community. And after that? The blasted woman was likely to have him starting to feel again. What the hell was happening to him? Everybody in the journalism profession knew that Richard Walton was a heartless son of a bitch.

He drew in a deep breath and stiffened his resolve. No sweet little temptress of a preacher was going to ruin him. He'd just have to find some way to prove to Anna Louise once and for all that he was a rotten bet.

"Is he going to help?" Maisey asked when Anna Louise stopped in the kitchen for a cup of tea.

"He sounded a little bit cranky, but in the end he said he would."

Maisey smiled and pulled her colorful afghan over her knees. "That's good, dear. Very good."

Anna Louise toyed with her spoon. "Maisey, why did Richard leave Kiley?"

"Haven't you asked him that?"

"Not really."

"He's the one who should tell you."

"But you know, don't you?"

"Of course, I know. There's very little about my grandson I don't understand. Leaving Kiley was something he had to do."

"Did he have a bad case of wanderlust?"

"I wouldn't say it was that so much. He just felt there was nothing for him here."

"You were here."

"And I loved him enough to let him go." Maisey got a faraway look in her eyes. "Now I wonder if maybe that wasn't a mistake. He left without ever settling things."

"Settling what things?"

"Anna Louise, you know I think of you as if you were part of my own family, but I can't tell you this. You'll have to ask Richard." She enfolded Anna Louise's hand in her own. "If you want him to stay, then you're going about it in exactly the right way. He needs to get to know the people of Kiley all over again, as an adult. Maybe now he'll see that they're only human and that human beings sometimes make dreadful mistakes that cause harm they never intended."

Anna Louise was shocked by the tears she saw gathering in Maisey's eyes. "Are you okay? I didn't mean to upset you."

"You didn't upset me. Not even the remembering did that. It's just the thought of all these wasted years." She pulled a hankie from her pocket and dabbed at her eyes. "Now, enough of that. It doesn't do a bit of good to shed tears over something that can't be changed. Tell me about the work you'll be doing tomorrow. How big will you make the recreation hall?"

Anna Louise gave in to the request reluctantly. She wanted badly to prod Maisey into telling her the whole story, but it wasn't in her nature to force anyone into revealing things before they were ready. Some in the church would say her patience was a weakness, but she didn't view it that way. Stirring folks into confessing sins before they'd come to terms with them didn't accomplish much. A little guilt and contemplation tended to make the eventual confession much more satisfying to the soul.

"If the weather's fine in the morning, you'll have to come and watch," she encouraged Maisey. "After all, this is going to be your recreation hall. You should approve of the way it's being built."

"That fancy architect from Charlottesville you sent by showed me the plans. I'm still not sure how you convinced him to volunteer his time to do the drawings."

Anna Louise grinned. "Maisey, don't you know by now that any preacher worth her salt has a silver tongue?"

Maisey's eyebrows lifted. "I thought you were only supposed to use that skill for divine purposes."

"Sometimes I like to test my limits and maybe broaden the definition of the phrase. Besides, Ted Bennett didn't require much convincing. I just reminded him about the night he tried to pick me up in a nightclub. He's been troubled ever since about his chances for getting into Heaven."

"Excuse me, but what were you doing in a nightclub in the first place?" Maisey teased.

"My best friend from college was getting married and we were holding her bachelorette party there. It was quite a celebration."

"No wonder this Mr. Bennett thought you were fair game."

"I did nothing to call attention to myself," Anna Louise informed her, then added thoughtfully, "then, again, it might have had something to do with the male stripper who jumped out of the cake."

Maisey's eyes widened. "Oh, my."

Anna Louise chuckled at her expression. "Sorry you missed it?"

"You bet I am. Any of your other friends planning to get married?"

"Afraid not. I'm the only one left who hasn't walked down the aisle."

"Your turn will come," Maisey told her firmly. Her expression turned mischievous. "And when it does, I think maybe I'll throw the party myself."

Richard was already at the site for the new recreation hall when Anna Louise arrived just after dawn with huge thermos bottles filled with hot coffee and bags of fresh doughnuts. With his hands shoved in his back pockets, he was standing next to Ted Bennett looking over the plans. His expression was skeptical.

Anna Louise handed the two men their coffee and offered them a doughnut. Neither of them took one. In fact, they barely even acknowledged her presence.

"Okay, what's the problem?" she finally asked. "You two are looking downright gloomy."

"This looks too damned complicated for a bunch of amateurs," Richard said.

"I thought you told me you were going to have experienced people on site," Ted added.

"You're experienced," she said to the dark-haired young man whose hands were clamped tightly around his coffee cup as if he needed its warmth.

"I'm an architect, not a contractor."

"Well, some of the people who'll be coming have building experience. Luke Hall, for instance."

"Aside from the shed where he stores his extra canned goods, what has Luke ever built?" Richard inquired.

"He built his own house," she snapped right back, losing patience with their negative attitudes.

Richard seemed startled by her statement and her tone. "I thought his house had been around for generations."

"The old one was. It burned down six years ago. I'm surprised Maisey didn't mention it to you."

He sighed. "Come to think of it, she might have," he admitted. "Okay, who else?"

"Hoyt Monroe has worked on a construction crew over in Charlottesville. And Nate Dorsey knows more about electricity than anyone in the whole valley. Nate said he'd bring along a friend who knows all about plumbing."

"Who's going to supervise?"

"I asked Billy Joe Hunt. He should be here any minute."

Richard went absolutely still. Anna Louise looked into his face and saw that his eyes were stone cold. "Do you have a problem with that?" she asked quietly.

"I thought he'd be dead by now."

"Billy Joe?" she repeated, shocked by his icy tone.

He shrugged. "The old coot deserved to die a long time ago."

Ted was listening to their exchange with an expression of growing alarm on his face. He looked as if he were ready to bolt. Anna Louise grabbed Richard's hand and dragged him away.

"Okay, why don't you tell me what this is all about?"

"It's past history, Anna Louise. Nothing for you to concern yourself about."

"If it's past history, then why did you look that way when I mentioned the man's name? Now you listen to me, Richard Walton. I don't know what you have against Billy Joe Hunt, but you bury it for the next forty-eight hours. I will not have some silly old grudge interfering with our ability to get this recreation hall built this weekend. Am I making myself clear?"

Something that might have been amusement flickered briefly in his eyes before he banked it. "You always do, Anna Louise. It must be nice to go through life with such clear-cut priorities."

With that, he turned his back on her and walked away.

She stared after him. "Now what the dickens was that all about?"

Chapter Nine

Richard rounded up Luke Hall and a few others and started work following the architect's directions. By the time the sun was high in the sky, the sound of nails being pounded echoed over the valley. There was a steady, satisfying rhythm to the noise.

The day once again had brought with it the warm temperatures of Indian summer. Sweat poured down his back and ran into his eyes as he worked. The hard labor kept him from thinking too much about Billy Joe Hunt, who had arrived a half hour before and started issuing orders like the controlling, domineering bastard he was.

Even though Richard knew that a number of people who knew their history were watching to see what would happen between him and Billy Joe, Richard couldn't seem to keep his eyes off the man. Billy Joe looked his age now, which had to be late fifties. He had a paunch from too much moonshine and too many barbecued ribs. His hair, which had gone gray over the past ten years, was clipped marine-cut short so that almost none showed beneath his baseball cap. His blustering, arrogant voice carried on the still morning air.

Only once had Billy Joe looked over to where Richard was working. Their gazes had clashed for no more than a heartbeat, but Richard had felt old hatreds welling up inside him. Swinging his hammer with vengeful force, he had split the next piece of wood he'd tried to hammer into place.

"Easy there," Luke had called over to him, his expression sympathetic. "I know you and Billy Joe have some things to work out, but today's not the time to go bringing it up. We're here to do a job."

Luke's placating tone irritated him. "You say it as if we squabbled over an old toy. Damn it, that man was single-handedly the cause of my mother's death," Richard blurted, his rage as fresh now as it had been some fifteen years earlier when he'd learned who'd been responsible for the cruel rumors that had destroyed his mother's will to live. "You can't honestly expect me to put that aside."

"Yes, I can," Luke said stubbornly. "Just for today, Richard. We've all got to pull together. Everybody in town knows what kind of bully Billy Joe Hunt is. He has a wicked tongue and a hard heart, but he does know how to build just about anything. That's why Anna Louise went to him. She knew we needed his expertise.''

Richard didn't want to hear what a paragon of building know-how Billy Joe was. "Too bad nobody seemed to recognize the rotten side of his nature fifteen years ago, when he made my mother the target," he retorted bitterly.

"There are a lot of people in Kiley who regret what happened back then. Many of them were too quick to judge Janie Walton."

"They believed a man like Billy Joe over her, just because he was a local boy and she was still considered an outsider even after living here for nearly fifteen years. My mother died because of the way she was shunned by everyone she'd thought of as friends and, not long after, my father gave up himself. It just took another two years for the depression to get so bad he killed himself."

He heard a sharply indrawn breath just then and looked around to see Anna Louise staring at him, an expression of horror on her face. Tears had welled up in her eyes. "I didn't know," she whispered. "If I'd known, I would never have called on him to help."

Richard fought for control over his temper. He didn't want to get into this with Anna Louise. He didn't want a lecture on forgiveness. "Like Luke said, it was a long time ago," he stated with cold matter-of-factness. "Let's get this recreation hall built and I'll deal with Billy Joe in my own way, in my own time."

"Please, tell me what happened," she begged.

He saw the compassion in her eyes, heard it in her voice, but he couldn't speak. The ache in his chest hurt too badly. "Not now, Anna Louise," he muttered gruffly. "Just keep him the hell away from me."

To Anna Louise's relief there were no confrontations between Richard and Billy Joe Hunt the rest of the day. Apparently fully aware that he could be the cause of a quick explosion of Richard's hair-trigger temper, Billy Joe had steered clear of him. Work on the recreation hall had proceeded at a brisk pace, with music blaring from radios and cheerful banter among the men.

Still, Anna Louise had kept a wary eye on Richard, worrying herself sick about the anger and hatred she had heard in his voice and even more about the anguish she had seen in his eyes. How could he ever expect to find peace inside himself, if he couldn't find forgiveness?

At least she finally had some inkling about what had driven him away from Kiley. She might not know all the details, but she knew enough to guess that he'd blamed the whole town for the loss of his parents and that he held Billy Joe Hunt responsible for stirring up whatever had happened.

When dusk fell, Richard was apparently the first to leave the building site. She looked everywhere for him as the others began making their way toward Tucker Patterson's store where chili and sandwiches had been prepared for the workers.

"Have you seen Richard?" she asked Luke Hall when he passed her on the road.

"Look for him out by Willow Creek," he suggested. "That's where he always used to go when he was hurting. I doubt that's changed."

Her heart heavy, Anna Louise walked up the hill to Maisey's, bypassing the house as she made her way to the creek behind it. As much as she would have liked to have Maisey's spin on things before she talked to Richard, Maisey had made it clear that any answers on this touchy subject would have to come from Richard himself.

A full moon, rising fast, lit the way. A breeze had picked up, chasing away the last of the Indian summer warmth and replacing it with bitter cold. She pulled her jacket more tightly around her and wished she'd thought to stop for a heavier coat and a scarf. Whatever shift there was to be in the weather, she just hoped the rain or snow would hold off until they could finish getting the roof on the recreation hall on Sunday afternoon after church services.

She found Richard sitting on the cold ground in the shadow of one of the willow trees, its branches bare now. "You're going to catch your death of cold out here," she said quietly.

"It wouldn't be much of a loss."

Anna Louise couldn't believe what she was hearing, not the words or the flat tone that said he meant them. "Richard Walton, how dare you! That is a terrible thing to say."

"Don't sound so shocked."

"I'm not shocked. I'm furious. I have never heard such hogwash coming from a supposedly intelligent man in my entire life."

"Are you saying you'd miss me, Anna Louise?"

She heard the unexpected note of laughter and something more, the faint slurring that suggested the bottle in his hand wasn't a soda as she had first assumed. "You're drunk." She was almost as astonished by that as she had been by his terrible claim that his life didn't matter.

"Not yet," he said carefully, "but I'm working on it."

She stood over him, hands on hips, practically trembling with indignation. "Well, that certainly makes a lot of sense. But then again, I suppose that's what I should have expected from a man who solves all of his problems by running away."

A hand shot up, caught hold of hers and yanked. Caught off guard, she tumbled straight into his lap. His breath was hot on her cheek when he asked in a lethal tone, "What the hell do you mean by that?"

She was too furious to be afraid. Only her good breeding and seminary training kept her from trying to pummel some sense into him.

"Just what I said," she retorted, looking him square in the eye. "You ran away from Kiley rather than dealing with whatever Billy Joe had done. You ran back here because you couldn't face what was going on in all those trouble spots you'd been assigned to cover. You ran to Washington when you thought you and I might be getting too close. Now you're running again, this time by staring into the bottom of a bottle. Haven't you figured out by now that running doesn't accomplish a blasted thing?''

His lips twitched in what might have been an attempt at a smile. "What makes you think I went to Washington to get away from you?" he said, startling her by picking that of all the accusations she'd made.

"I saw how you looked after you kissed me. It scared you, didn't it, Mr. Hotshot Reporter? I know you did it on some kind of macho lark, but it didn't turn out the way you expected, did it? You're real brave when it comes to facing down some petty tyrant in a foreign land, but a small-town preacher scares you to death.''

He didn't respond, but his hands circled her waist and tried to pin her in place. When she tried to wriggle free, he muttered, "Damn, woman, would you hold still?''

"I will not," she snapped back.

"Sweetheart, I don't think you're prepared to deal with the consequences," he taunted in a low, dry tone.

She glowered at him. "And what consequences would those be?''

He shifted slightly and chuckled at the shock that spread over her face when she caught on to what he meant. "Oh, my," she whispered, stunned by the discovery that he was thoroughly aroused by her squirming, their battle of wits, or some combination of the two.

"Indeed," he said.

Anna Louise froze right where she was, afraid to move a muscle. She'd meant to taunt him out of his dark mood, not to provoke him into a seduction. She had to admit, though, that she was fascinated by the discovery that she could have that effect on him. No wonder Jeremy and Maribeth had such difficulty with the concept of chastity, if this was the temptation they faced.

Nothing in her entire previous experience had prepared her for the wicked way she felt. In high school and college she'd been single-minded about meeting her goal of becoming a pastor. If men had been attracted to her, she'd been blind to it. And even though she'd been surrounded by men in seminary, she'd been more interested in proving something to them than dating them. Richard was the first man who'd raised her carnal awareness to such a feverish pitch. Before, she'd always felt contented. Since he'd come into her world, she'd felt alive.

"Let me go, you cretin. You're not getting out of a discussion of your cowardly behavior by using sex to intimidate me." To her chagrin, she was reacting exactly the way she'd just accused Richard of behaving. She was running scared.

Richard smirked, but he did release her. Anna Louise scrambled to her feet and stood a few careful feet away. "Well?" she prodded.

"Well, what?"

"What do you have to say for yourself?"

"Nothing."

She stared at him. How could a person carry on a decent argument, if the other person refused to fight back? "Nothing? You have to say something."

"Why?" he inquired, his tone suddenly extraordinarily reasonable.

Anna Louise again had an intense desire to smack him. What on earth was happening to her? She was a peaceful woman, not a brawler. "You are the most infuriating man it has ever been my misfortune to meet, Richard Walton."

"I don't doubt it."

"You don't have to sound so darned pleased about it."

"Anna Louise, has it occurred to you that this conversation is moving in circles? Frankly, it's making me dizzy."

"That's not the conversation, it's the liquor," she snapped back. "If you'd throw away that bottle, we could have a serious talk." She made a grab for the bottle, but he held it out of reach.

"Exactly what would you like to talk about?"

"I want to know what happened here fifteen years ago."

"Now that," he said softly, but emphatically, "is something I don't intend to discuss."

"Coward," she accused.

"You keep calling me that, sweetheart. It's beginning to lose its effectiveness."

Anna Louise sighed. "Can't you see I just want to help?"

"I don't doubt it for a minute, but this is way beyond something you can fix with a sympathetic ear and a gentle touch. Not everything in life can be fixed, Anna Louise. Now that's the gospel truth."

"I don't believe that. I think prayer can help a person to heal, if only they'll listen to God's answers."

"Do you think I haven't prayed about this, Pastor Perkins?" he taunted, his voice thick with sarcasm. "Do you think when I was fourteen years old and my sad, lonely mama was wandering around in a blizzard because she didn't have a single friend in this terrible place, do you think I didn't pray then? Do you think I didn't get on my knees and pray when she was in her bed dying of pneumonia? Well, let me correct that impression. I got on my knees and I said every prayer I'd been taught from the day I was born," he said angrily.

"My daddy prayed. Maisey prayed. And do you know what happened, Pastor Perkins? She died, anyway. That sweet, gentle woman, who'd never done anybody any harm, died, and all because Billy Joe Hunt made it his personal quest to destroy her with his lies and innuendos about her past. She couldn't face the humiliation and she wasn't strong enough to fight back."

Anna Louise felt the force of his fury and wanted desperately to comfort him. But comfort wasn't what he needed now. He needed to tear open this festering wound, to get out all of the hurt and anguish that were killing him bit by bit, and find his own path to forgiveness. She could only guide him along the way.

"What was it Billy Joe did?"

"He told people . . ." For a minute it didn't seem as if he would say any more, but he finally went on. "He told people a lot of nonsense about the way she'd been living over in Charlottesville before she and my daddy met."

"Was it true?"

"Does that really matter? Whatever had gone on had been over with for fifteen years. How Billy Joe dug up his little half-truths and lies about her living with some professor, I can't imagine. But I don't care if she'd been the worst prostitute in history—which she hadn't been, by the way. She deserved the chance to put the past behind her. He had to go dragging it all up, implying that she'd slept with half the damned campus, humiliating her, making her feel unwelcome everywhere." Richard glared up at her. "Even in *your* blessed church."

Anna Louise recalled that the previous preacher, Pastor Flynn, had had a reputation for being rigid and cold. She'd had no idea how hard-hearted he'd actually been. If he had actually driven away Richard's mother, then his sin was far worse than any Janie Walton might have committed.

"That was wrong," she said quietly.

"You're damned right, it was wrong. What Billy Joe did was wrong. Half the people in this town were wrong for following his lead."

"Does knowing that help?" she asked quietly.

He shot a startled look up at her. "What do you mean?"

"It's a simple question. I'm asking if it makes you feel better to hold them all responsible for your mother's death. Does hating them all give you any satisfaction?"

"Yes," he said fiercely. Then he released a deep sigh. "No. No, it doesn't help at all."

She knelt down beside him, mindless of the cold, hard ground. She rested her hand against his cheek, which was damp with the silent tears she hadn't even been aware he'd shed. "Then isn't it time to let it go?"

"I can't."

"Why not?"

He met her gaze, his expression bleak. "Because if I do, I'll have nothing left."

Anna Louise felt her own tears spill down her cheeks. "That's not true. It's not. You have Maisey." She drew in a deep breath. "And you have me."

His gaze met hers, his eyes dark with heartache and need. With a groan, he pulled her into his arms and held her tight against his chest. Slowly he rocked back and forth, as if in the rhythm and closeness he could find the solace he desperately needed. Anna Louise twined her arms around his neck and held on tight, afraid to let go for fear of losing him forever.

They were still sitting just that way when the first flakes of snow began to fall, melting against their skin. Anna Louise lifted her head in wonder.

"The first snowfall," she whispered. "It's always the most beautiful."

Richard's low chuckle was the first sign she'd had that his mood had finally shifted. "Anna Louise, is there anything in life you don't view as a blessing?"

"I'm not overly fond of asparagus," she responded, just to see the grin on his face broaden.

"Oh, Anna Louise, you are a treasure," he said, laughing.

Anna Louise realized a few weeks later that that intimate moment she had shared with Richard wasn't the beginning she had hoped it might be. His pattern was too well established. After losing both his parents during his teens, he had never allowed another soul to get too close. He'd even run as far as he could from Maisey. Maybe, though, his coming home when she needed him was the first step in his recovery. Facing down the demon of Billy Joe Hunt and his awful lies might be the next.

That, however, didn't solve the immediate problem of his avoiding any possible contact with Anna Louise. Oh, he was polite enough when they bumped into each other on the street. He was even courteous when Maisey invited Anna Louise to join them for dinner, which she did as frequently as ever.

Anna Louise tried to avoid those tension-filled occasions, but Maisey would only accept so many excuses before she figured out what was really going on. Anna Louise didn't want to stir up trouble between Richard and his grandmother by hinting that he'd in any way made her feel unwelcome.

Thanksgiving came and went. Plans for the annual Christmas bazaar were keeping everyone busy. Like similar bazaars in Europe, theirs was held outdoors, with booths selling hot chocolate, crafts, holiday decorations and baked goods. People came from as far away as Charlottesville to stock up on unique Christmas items. Maisey's crocheted pieces were always a big hit, but this year she'd said she didn't feel up to sitting outside in the cold weather to run her own booth. She'd cajoled Richard into doing it for her.

Anna Louise passed by several times and saw that he'd found plenty of company. She had the most uncharitable desire to claw Penelope King's eyes out. Richard's old high school sweetheart seemed fairly determined to win him back and he didn't seem to be fighting her.

Losing her holiday spirit entirely, Anna Louise slipped away and went into the house. The flashing light on her answering machine taunted her from clear across the room. Her breath seemed to catch in her throat.

"Not again," she whispered, staring at the machine as if it had taken on a life of its own.

A highly developed sense of responsibility prevented her from ignoring that flashing light. It could have been important, one of her parishioners in need of her comfort. But she knew in her gut what she'd hear when she pressed the play button.

"Enjoy it while you can," the voice whispered with malicious glee. "Your days are running out. When the council vote is taken, your church will be taken away from you and you will be just another sinner."

Anna Louise sank down into a chair beside the desk and slowly pressed the button to erase the message. She listened to the whir of the tape taking away the vitriolic words, but it brought her no real relief. It was impossible to erase the awareness that there was someone in Kiley who hated her just for being who she was, who was so determined to destroy her and everything she'd worked for.

"Anna Louise?"

She looked up and saw the concern written all over Richard's face.

"Are you okay? You're white as a sheet."

"I'm fine," she insisted.

He glanced at the answering machine, which was now silent and unblinking. "Bad news?" he guessed.

She drew herself up and forced a smile. "No. Just something I'm going to have to deal with one of these days. I'd hoped it wouldn't be quite this soon."

"Am I supposed to know what that means?"

"No. Sorry." She managed to inject a cheerful note into her voice by sheer force of will. "How are Maisey's crocheted items going?"

"All sold out."

"She'll be pleased."

"I just have one question," he admitted conspiratorially, his mood lighter than it had been in weeks. "What the hell were they, anyway?"

Anna Louise chuckled. "Doilies, for the most part."

"What do you do with them?"

"Aren't there any in her house?" she asked, then answered her own question. "That's right. She doesn't have any. She said she didn't feel like washing them and starching them anymore."

He continued to look bewildered. "They can't be coasters, because the water would go right through all those little holes. Besides, they're too big. I don't get it."

"They go on tables. Sometimes on the arms of the sofa."

"What for?"

"Decoration."

He nodded sagely. "That explains why she doesn't have any at home. They're tacky."

Anna Louise winced. "For goodness' sakes, don't say that around here. You've just sold them to half the people at the bazaar."

His eyes sparkled with mischief. "I know. Just proves my point."

"Richard!" she protested, biting back a laugh.

"Don't worry, Anna Louise, I won't tell, if you don't."

She studied his expression for a minute. "You just said all that to get me to laugh, didn't you?"

He winked at her. "Worked, didn't it?" His expression sobered. "I just wish you'd tell me why you were so upset in the first place."

She couldn't get into it with him. The call would just reaffirm everything he already felt about the narrow-mindedness of people in Kiley. She leveled a perfectly serious look at him.

"Maybe I was just upset because you ran out of those doilies before I could get one," she said, and took off before he could probe any more deeply.

Chapter Ten

If December's weather was any indication, Richard didn't want any part of January and February in Kiley. There had been two significant snowstorms already and the temperature had dipped close to zero on more nights than he cared to count. Not even a fire that blazed day and night had been able to ward off the chill in Maisey's drafty old house. He'd taken to wearing so many layers of clothes, it took him ten solid minutes just to undress for bed. So much for spontaneous sex, he thought with a wry grimace.

Not that sex was much of an issue, not with the only woman on his mind being Anna Louise. He'd done everything he could to steer clear of her whenever possible, but the efforts had been useless.

Not even the very willing Penelope had been able to distract him. He'd finally explained gently that he had no intention of getting involved with her again while he was in Kiley. He didn't say that Anna Louise's image was with him when he went to bed at night and with him when he woke up in the morning. He didn't explain that while he slept, it was Anna Louise who tormented him in his dreams with her unintentionally sexy ways and her unavailability.

He told himself that her being unavailable was what made him unable to shake her loose. If he'd been able to satisfy this fascination with an uncomplicated roll in the hay, he'd be over her by now. Unfortunately, that was out of the question, even though he saw definite signs of willingness in her eyes from time to time. Willing or not, there could be nothing uncomplicated about sleeping with Anna Louise.

He was still tucked under the layers of comforters considering his options when he heard Maisey coughing. The dry, hacking sound practically shook the house and brought him to his feet. He yanked on his clothes and tore down the hall.

"Are you all right?" he demanded from the doorway to her room.

"Fine," she insisted, then went into another spasm of coughs.

Richard plunked himself down on the side of the bed and glared at her. "Maisey, I don't want you to even think about getting out of this bed today. I'm calling Doc Benson."

"Nonsense. I'll be fit as a fiddle as soon as I get a cup of tea into me. Would you mind making it this morning?"

He cast one last worried look at her as he stood up. "I'll bring you some juice, too. And maybe a little honey for the tea. Is your throat sore?"

"Just a mite. The tea will fix me right up."

In the kitchen, Richard put the kettle on for tea, then placed a call to the doctor. Before he could think better of it, he made another call, this one to Anna Louise. Just the sound of her voice made his pulse pick up speed.

"Anna Louise, could you stop by sometime today? It's Maisey. I'm worried about her."

"Have you called Doc Benson?"

"He'll be by within the hour."

"I have to make another call, but I'll be there as soon as I can."

He was pleased by her matter-of-fact response. There was no hysteria. Anna Louise was a woman who had the kind of strength it took to handle almost anything. She'd be a real comfort in a crisis.

Exactly the sort of woman a man who courted danger needed by his side. The thought crept in before he could stop it. He dismissed it at once, then wondered at the fact that he'd instinctively turned to her this morning. He tried to convince himself he'd done it for Maisey's sake, knowing how she always responded to Anna Louise's gentle touch and quiet prayers. He knew better, though. He'd also done it because he wanted her there for himself, just in case this cough of Maisey's turned out to be something serious.

It startled him some that a man who'd faced sniper fire and pestilence without a qualm could come unglued when faced with no more than a hacking cough. But it was Maisey's cough, he reminded himself. And he'd always cared more about what happened to his grandmother than he'd ever worried about himself. In retrospect he realized that was probably why he'd left her behind for so long. He'd been bracing himself against the possibility of losing her.

Forty-five minutes later Anna Louise turned up, just as Doc Benson was finishing his examination. Richard was pacing the kitchen, trying not to panic at Maisey's terrible, dry cough, which seemed to have worsened. His spirits picked up some at the sight of Anna Louise, with her hair all windblown and untidy and her cheeks flushed from the icy air.

"Get over here by the fire," he insisted, "before you catch your death of cold, too." Too many bad memories of a winter just like this lingered for him to ever be able to take survival of the elements for granted again.

"How is she?" Anna Louise asked, rubbing her hands together briskly as she held them over the heat.

Just then Maisey coughed again. The sound was so wrenching, Richard couldn't imagine how her frail body lasted through it.

"It's getting worse," he told her. "It wasn't that bad even an hour ago. Is this Benson guy any good?

Maybe I should call for a specialist to come in from Washington."

"I doubt you'd get one to make a house call clear down here. Besides, Jonathan Benson is a fine doctor. He went to Harvard and interned at Johns Hopkins."

"Then what's he doing way out here in the boondocks?"

"He wanted to practice family medicine." She put her hands on his shoulders and waited until he met her gaze. "Maisey is in very capable hands. Now, stop worrying."

"If you say so," he muttered, and resumed his pacing.

It was another fifteen minutes before Doc Benson emerged, his expression sober, but not exactly grim. Richard dared to hope. "Is she okay?"

"With that cough?" Benson said dryly. "Hardly. But I've given her some medicine that should ease the cough and break up the congestion in her chest. I'll send Tucker Patterson out with more. If she's not better in a day or two, you'll have to think about taking her to the hospital. I don't want any more strain on her heart."

"I'll take her today, if that's what's best for her."

"No. She was adamant about staying here. If you can keep her in that bed, then I'll go along with it."

"She'll stay there," Richard said with grim determination.

"I'll go in and sit with her awhile," Anna Louise said.

When the doctor had gone and with Anna Louise in with Maisey, Richard finally had to admit to himself the flash of terror he'd felt earlier when he'd thought Maisey might be seriously ill. He couldn't lose her, too. She was all he had. He'd stayed away for years, hoping that she would come to matter less and less, preparing himself for the eventuality of losing her. It hadn't worked. He'd finally realized he should be treasuring whatever time they had left together, not anticipating the loneliness of the time when she would be gone. Once again, he had to face the fact that he had no business going overseas again.

He poured himself a cup of coffee and sank into a rocker in front of the fire. He was still there, lost in thought, when Anna Louise finally tiptoed out of Maisey's room.

"She's sleeping."

He stood and moved closer to the fire. "I couldn't bear to lose her," he said, his voice catching. He couldn't meet Anna Louise's gaze.

"You will someday. You have to face that."

"Not now."

She came up behind him and wrapped her arms around his waist. "I wish you shared my faith," she said, her head resting against his back.

He drew comfort from her nearness, if not from her words. "If you'd been where I've been, seen what I've seen. . . ."

"We may not understand it, but there is always a purpose to everything that happens. If you can't accept that for yourself, then at least know that Maisey does believe it. She is at peace with whatever God has in store for her.''

Anger bubbled up inside him, but he forced it back. Rage was pointless. He sighed and turned to face her, his arms now circling her in a loose embrace. ''Thank you for reminding me of that. It's selfish of me to need any more.''

Anna Louise shook her head, a faint smile tugging at her mouth. ''Not selfish, Richard, just human. You've spent too long thinking of yourself as some larger-than-life hero, living recklessly and challenging fate. The fact of the matter is, though, that you're simply human, just like the rest of us.''

Richard wondered what Anna Louise with her lofty talk and gentle ways would say if she realized exactly how human he felt right this minute with her in his arms and what a struggle he was going to have letting her go.

Two weeks later, that rare, special moment of intimacy with Anna Louise and his own fears for Maisey's health had practically faded from Richard's memory. His grandmother's returning vitality had wiped away his panic and determination had quieted any thoughts of Anna Louise.

Well, practically any thoughts. She still popped into his head at the most inconvenient times, taunting him with memories of her warmth and generosity of spirit. No question about it, Anna Louise lived the kind of life she preached about. There was no room in that life for a renegade journalist who was filled with bitterness.

Or so he told himself time and again when temptation seemed about to get the better of him.

"You're not dressed," Maisey said just then as she came into the kitchen where Richard was sitting in his favorite chair by the fire.

He glanced up from the new book on foreign policy that had come in the morning mail. It had been sent by his boss with a curt note suggesting he immerse himself in research for his next assignment "assuming you expect to get back to work this century." He hadn't read a word of the thick tome in the past hour. That alone was a testament to the way his priorities had shifted in the past few months.

"Dressed for what?" he said.

"Christmas Eve service." She frowned at him. "Don't look at me that way, young man. I've been going to this service since I was a girl and I don't intend to stop now."

"Maisey, you've been in bed for the past two weeks. It's too blasted cold for you to be traipsing around the countryside. You'll catch pneumonia." It was not an idle worry, given her recent state of health. He'd seen a far younger, stronger woman succumb in weather just like this.

"We're driving five minutes in a car with heat you keep turned up like an old blast furnace. I'll be fine." She regarded him slyly. "Of course, if you insist on staying here, I'll have to walk. It's too late to call one of the neighbors to pick me up."

Richard sighed in resignation. "Give me ten minutes," he said, and reluctantly went to put on a suit.

As he changed clothes, he thought about the way he'd spent the previous Christmas. He'd been holed up in a hotel with a dozen other journalists, listening to the shelling that hadn't let up for the holiday. Supplies were scarce, but a British reporter who'd recently arrived had brought along a fresh supply of Scotch whiskey. The overall mood was increasingly mellow, but hardly filled with holiday cheer.

Then an Italian correspondent had gotten word that a church in town was holding a Christmas Eve service despite the dangerous chaos in the streets. They had bundled up, then traipsed on foot over the icy roads to report on the bravery and determination of people who refused to let a war keep them from worshiping on this holiest of nights.

He could remember distinctly the sharp bite of the wind, the achingly cold dampness that had penetrated through layers of wool, then the faint, beckoning flicker of candlelight in the windows of the ancient church. Even more clearly, he remembered the constant *rat-a-tat-tat* of gunfire.

To his astonishment, the pews had been filled. The scent of evergreens and incense had mingled in air that was almost as cold indoors as it had been outside. Voices rose in harmony over unfamiliar prayers in a language he barely understood.

He recalled with vivid clarity his sense that the prayers were wasted. Rather than seeing the poignancy and hope in the church that night, he had thought only of the folly. The sense that those suffering such terrible hardships were placing their faith in an uncaring God had never seemed clearer.

Discovering in the morning that half a dozen people, two of them children, had been killed on their way home from that service solidified his sense that prayers were useless against insanity. That conviction had never left him.

Tonight, though, he pushed aside his own cynicism as a gift to Maisey. Going to this service was important to her and he could not let her down. With each passing day he had grown more aware of her increasing frailty. There was no way to tell how many more Christmases she might have. If a church service brought her comfort, then he owed it to her not to spoil that.

Outside, the clear sky looked as if diamonds had been scattered across it. The moon cast streams of silver across the landscape. Not a single sound disrupted the utter stillness. The quiet, which should have soothed, instead seemed almost unnatural after years of spending Christmas in places where the chilling sound of gunfire was more prevalent than that of joyous carols. Even when an official truce had been called, there were always those who violated it.

Tonight, though, in this place, the peace was real, the silence unbroken. His heart skipped a beat when he spotted Anna Louise greeting the arrivals on the steps of the church. Her cheeks were pink from the brisk night air and her eyes were bright with an excitement that stirred a matching sense of anticipation in him. A warm smile spread across her face at the sight of Maisey, then faded. Worry puckered her forehead.

"Should you be out of bed?" she asked.

"Exactly what I said," Richard told her.

"This is my favorite service of the year," Maisey told them both, her chin set stubbornly. "Now you two stop pestering me and let me enjoy it."

Richard's gaze caught Anna Louise's. She grinned at him. "At least get her inside where it's warm. There will be hot chocolate and cookies at my place afterward. Will you join us?"

"Have you ever known me to miss a party?" Maisey retorted before Richard could get in a word. She tugged on his arm. "Let's find a seat before they're all taken."

Inside the church, pine boughs and red ribbon had been used to decorate the ends of the pews. Thick white candles burned at the front of the church, their soft glow creating an atmosphere of quiet serenity.

They had been seated for no more than a couple of minutes when Mabel Hartley struck the first chords of "Joy to the World" on the piano. The choir led the congregation in the familiar carol. Maisey's sweet soprano carried above the others. Even to Richard's jaded ears, the sound was joyous. He listened for Anna Louise's deeper, richer tones but couldn't detect her voice amid all the others. He felt a sharp nudge from Maisey's elbow.

"Sing," she muttered when he glanced down at her. She lifted her hymnal so he could see the words.

At first he resisted, but his grandmother was watching him so hopefully that he finally began to mouth the once-familiar refrain. They went through the same thing with each carol. Richard stood stiff and silent, until Maisey poked him in the side. Then he at least formed the words, lip-synching along, regretting that he couldn't recapture the feelings of wonder and anticipation that he had once felt as a boy on Christmas Eve.

The talk of peace on earth, goodwill toward men seemed like an empty refrain to him.

Slowly, though, the carols and passages of Scripture carried him back to another time in his life, a time when his parents had been alive and happy and anything had seemed possible. The hard knot in his chest began to ease.

By the time the service ended with Anna Louise's clear voice singing the opening notes of "Silent Night," an unfamiliar sensation seemed to be creeping through him. He realized with a sense of amazement that what he was feeling was a rare moment of absolute contentment.

Anna Louise stood in the doorway to the kitchen, listening to the laughter of her congregation, watching the excited children slowly give in to exhaustion. These people had become her family over the past few years. They had welcomed her. At times, they had tested and challenged her. On occasion, they had frustrated and angered her. But always, they had filled her heart with their basic generosity and kindness. The people of Kiley were good people. She wondered if she would be with them this time next year.

"Why so sad?" Richard asked, coming up beside her.

"Just thinking ahead."

"Afraid you'll find only coal in your stocking tomorrow morning?"

She met his laughing gaze. "You're the one who ought to be worrying about that. You're much naughtier than I am."

"We could change that."

Anna Louise sighed, the sound a mixture of longing and regret. "You know we can't," she said, her voice far too wistful.

"Would the people of Kiley be appalled if I gave you a Christmas kiss? You are standing right here under the mistletoe, you know."

She thought of how she had imagined just such a kiss when she'd hung the mistletoe in the doorway. A carefree, innocent kiss. Fat chance. If Richard Walton kissed her, mistletoe or not, there would be nothing innocent about it. She knew from past experience the man would curl her toes. And she would be left with enough forbidden desires—that didn't include marriage—to condemn her to Hell. She'd be on her knees praying for forgiveness from now until next Easter.

When she finally looked into Richard's face again, she caught the amusement.

"If I had to guess, I'd say you took the idea of that kiss and ran with it," he taunted.

"I was just weighing the benefits with the alternative."

"Which is?"

"Eternal damnation."

"For a kiss?"

"For what you and I both know would likely come after," she said with blunt candor.

"Why, Miss Anna Louise, I can control my baser instincts, if you can."

His playful mood charmed her, dared her to take chances. "Maybe that's the problem. A man like you is pure temptation to a woman like me."

His expression sobered for an instant. "And I have no business teasing you the way I do, do I?"

"No," she admitted.

"Want me to stop?"

Her gaze clashed with his and her breath caught in her throat at the hint of desire she saw in his eyes. Because she couldn't manage even a single word, she mutely shook her head. She would not, could not, deny herself this one instant of feeling outrageously desirable.

She felt his fingers against her cheek, just a whisper of a touch that sent heat and longing swirling through her.

"Merry Christmas, Anna Louise," he said softly.

"Merry Christmas, Richard."

With that, the sweetest temptation she had ever known walked out the door, his grandmother right behind him.

* * *

The memory of that brief, tender moment stayed with Anna Louise all night long. Sometime toward dawn she recognized that what she was feeling toward Richard Walton wasn't just some yearning to help him. It wasn't a professional desire to save his jaded soul. No, what she was feeling was much more personal. She was falling in love with him.

Over the past months she had looked beneath that hard, cynical surface and found the man who cared so deeply that the agony in other parts of the world had irreparably hurt him. Watching him with Maisey, she had caught glimpses of the warmth and generosity he tried so hard to pretend didn't exist. And she sensed that untapped within him was an unlimited capacity to love, if only someone was willing to work hard enough to cut through the barriers he'd erected.

The discovery that she wanted desperately to be that person left her trembling with anticipation and terror. She knew instinctively that he wouldn't thank her for her efforts. He'd convinced himself that he wanted quick and easy relationships. She represented trouble. Richard would figure complications and commitment went hand-in-hand with any sort of relationship with her.

Of course, that worked both ways. A man determined to avoid commitment, a man dead set against putting down roots, was not exactly a good bet for a church pastor. Anna Louise guessed that the realization she'd come to overnight about the depth of her feelings pretty much guaranteed trouble on her horizon, as well. What would happen when Richard eventually left on another assignment? How would she be able to bear the loneliness? How could she stand the worry Maisey must have endured all these years?

Because she wanted a clear head, she walked instead of driving up the hill to Maisey's for Christmas dinner. Her teeth were chattering and she was chilled to the bone by the time she reached the house. The smoke curling from the chimney promised coziness, but it was the image of Richard waiting inside that warmed her before she ever set foot across the threshold.

"Come in, come in," Maisey called, holding the door wide. "I think we'll have more snow before the day's out, don't you?"

"It feels that way," Anna Louise agreed.

"Did you walk all this way? Richard could have come to get you."

"No, I wanted the exercise and fresh air."

Maisey gave her a kiss on the cheek. "Merry Christmas, dear. Let's get you in by the fire, so you can warm up before dinner."

"Let me help."

"Nonsense. The turkey's almost done. The pie's already out of the oven. All that's left is mashing the potatoes. It won't take me a minute to do that."

Anna Louise drew in a deep breath. "It smells wonderful."

"It's even nicer in the parlor. Richard cut a fresh tree for me day before yesterday. Come along and see."

With an odd mix of reluctance and anticipation, Anna Louise followed Maisey into the living room expecting to find Richard. He was nowhere in sight.

Apparently Maisey caught her disappointment. "He's gone for a walk. He said he needed the cold air to blow away the cobwebs."

Anna Louise wondered if that was a euphemism for the same troubling thoughts that had pestered her all night long and had sent her crunching over the icy road to Maisey's on foot. Served him right for taunting her the night before.

When he finally did turn up, the familiar glint of amusement was still in his eyes, along with that blatant hint of desire that made her pulse buck.

"It's about time," Maisey scolded him. "We have presents to open and you know I have no patience." She reached for a large package under the tree and handed it to Anna Louise. "I thought it would be nice with your coloring."

Anna Louise's fingers trembled under the intensity of Richard's gaze as she tried to undo the ribbons on the box. Finally, she just ripped the wrappings away with unladylike enthusiasm.

Inside she found a shawl knit of the softest wool she'd ever touched. "Maisey, did you make this?" she said, holding the pale peach material up to her cheek.

"My mother did. I've been saving it all these years for somebody special. I want you to have it."

Anna Louise felt the salty sting of tears. "Oh, Maisey, you are so sweet. My gift for you isn't nearly this wonderful."

"Your friendship is gift enough for me," Maisey assured her, but her expression was as excited as a child's when she opened the small box Anna Louise handed her. She folded open the tissue paper and found a framed photo of Richard that Anna Louise had taken on the day they had worked on the recreation hall. It had been shot in a rare instant when his chiseled features were softened by a smile.

"It's perfect," Maisey enthused. "Darling, you look downright handsome. I'll put this right up here on the mantel."

"You took that?" Richard said, a spark of mischief in his eyes.

Anna Louise nodded.

"Caught me when I wasn't looking, I see." He grinned at her. "Did you keep a copy for your bedside?"

Anna Louise blushed furiously because she'd been sorely tempted to do just that. "I did not!"

"Remind me to have a look later."

"Richard Walton, the odds of you getting anywhere near my bedroom are between slim and none."

"We'll see," he taunted as Maisey laughed with obvious delight at the bantering.

"Having the two of you here," Maisey said softly, "it's the best Christmas in a very long time."

Anna Louise glanced over at Richard, taking in the sight of him looking so relaxed and carefree for the first time since she'd known him. If only it could always be like this, she thought.

If only...

Chapter Eleven

An odd sense of contentment, begun in the church on Christmas Eve, stayed with Richard through Christmas dinner. Maisey, while still fragile, seemed happier than ever. Having Anna Louise around guaranteed that there would be laughter.

He patted his pocket, feeling the gift he'd tucked away there with the intention of giving it to Anna Louise when they had a moment alone. He hadn't been able to resist the sterling silver combs he'd seen in an antique shop one afternoon. The moment he'd spotted them, he'd envisioned them holding back the fiery strands of her untamable red hair.

There was no doubt the opportunity for giving them to her would arise. Maisey would see to that. If there was one thing in life he could count on, it was his grandmother's matchmaking. At times it still astonished him that she seemed to see nothing odd about pairing a renegade like him with Anna Louise. She actually seemed to think he was good enough for a parson.

Obviously his grandmother couldn't see into his wicked heart and detect the lust that had lodged there from the first time he'd ever set eyes on Anna Louise. Or maybe Maisey was even better than he was at putting spin on a story. Maybe she was calling it love.

Whatever, he thought with a small measure of guilt. He'd suddenly decided to snatch whatever time he could with Anna Louise, storing up the peace and calm she inspired in him for the troubled days that no doubt lay in his future once he went back to reporting. He would take that from her, but not her innocence. He'd made himself a solemn promise about that. She might hurt when he left. There might be no way around that. But he would see to it she would not suffer from guilt and regrets.

"Another piece of pumpkin pie?" Maisey suggested.

"Not for me," Anna Louise replied. "I feel as if I ate that entire turkey all by myself."

"You couldn't have," Richard countered. "I ate most of it."

"That must explain why all I had was that piddly little wing," Maisey teased. "If you don't want any more dessert, how about more coffee?"

"No. I really should be getting home," Anna Louise said. "I want to call my family before it gets to be too late. My parents should be back from my sister's by now. Everyone was planning to spend the holiday with her in Memphis so they could see the new baby."

Richard watched her closely and thought he detected a trace of wistfulness in her expression. "Are you feeling homesick?"

"Maybe just a little," she admitted with a sigh. "I wonder if I'll ever get used to not being at home for the holidays."

"But, dear," Maisey said gently, "you are home."

Anna Louise suddenly smiled as if she'd just been given another gift. "Yes, I am, aren't I? Thank you for reminding me of that."

"Are you sure you need to leave?" Maisey asked, her expression radiating disappointment.

"Yes. I want to make that call and you need to get some rest. I know how much effort goes into preparing a meal like the one we had."

"Hey, what makes you think *I* wasn't responsible for the turkey and stuffing?" Richard demanded.

"Maisey's described your pitiful cooking skills to me."

"All lies."

"I've seen the evidence for myself. Remember that entire loaf of bread you burned trying to make toast?"

He laughed. "Ssh. You weren't supposed to tell Maisey about that."

Maisey chuckled. "Did you honestly think I couldn't smell all that burning bread? I worried we'd never get the smell out of the house, to say nothing of whether you'd remember where I keep the fire extinguisher."

Richard feigned a scowl at the pair of them. "And here I was about to volunteer to walk Anna Louise home." He glanced across the room and saw the color rise in Anna Louise's cheeks at the suggestion.

"Really, it's not necessary," she protested.

"Yes, it is," Maisey insisted. "You can argue with Richard, but you shouldn't upset an old lady."

"Maisey, you're not old," Anna Louise said. "You're going to outlive all of us."

"I just hope I'll be around long enough to see my grandson happily married and maybe my first great-grandbaby." She shot a pointed look straight at Richard. "There's not a lot of time to waste, young man."

He leaned down and pressed a kiss on her cheek. "Some things just can't be rushed."

"Rushed? You're slower than molasses."

Richard looked at Anna Louise. "I think we'd better get out of here before she calls Orville Patterson over to perform the ceremony."

Outside, he tucked Anna Louise's arm through his. "Don't let Maisey's teasing bother you."

"I'm not the one she's pestering to get married."

"That's what you think," he retorted.

They took their time walking over the packed snow, partly because the footing was treacherous and partly to draw the time out. The moon showed them the way. Richard glanced up the side of the mountain and saw half a dozen kids with their sleds racing down the slope, their excited shouts carrying on the night air. He glanced at Anna Louise and saw that she'd seen them, as well.

"I dare you," he teased.

Her gaze flew up to his. "You've got to be kidding. I haven't been sledding in years."

"Neither have I."

"But you're a daredevil. I'm not."

"That gleam in your eyes says otherwise."

"We don't have sleds."

"Oh, I think we can talk those kids into loaning us two for one run down the hill." He grinned at the temptation that was written plainly all over her face. "You game?"

Her thoughtful gaze remained pinned on the laughing children for another minute, then she grinned. "Let's go for it."

At the top of the hill, Richard spoke to the two youngest Hall boys and borrowed their sleds.

"Are you really going to race him, Pastor Perkins?" sixteen-year-old Jason Hall asked, his eyes wide.

Anna Louise looked startled. "Who said anything about a race?"

Richard trained his most innocent expression on her. "Afraid of a little competition?"

"No, I'm afraid of breaking my neck," she said as she settled herself cautiously on the sled.

Richard shot a conspiratorial look at the gathered kids and gave her sled a gentle nudge.

"Why you lousy..." she shouted as the sled began its rapid descent.

"Tsk-tsk, Pastor Perkins," he called out as he hopped on his own sled and sent it racing down the slope after her.

"How do you steer the blasted thing?" she shouted with a note of alarm in her voice.

Richard suffered a moment's absolute panic at the thought that she really might not know what she was doing. An image of her slamming into a tree flashed through his head with sickening clarity. Dear Heaven, what had he done?

Concern had him trying to maneuver himself into her path, so he could save her. Only when she whooshed by, her laughter carried on the crisp night air, did he realize he'd been had.

At the bottom of the hill, when he caught up with her, she was still laughing.

"You deliberately distracted me," he accused, tumbling her from the sled into the snow and pinning her down, his body pressed intimately against hers.

"You're the one who insisted on a race," she reminded him, her eyes sparkling with mischief.

"I expected a *fair* race."

The kids arrived just then, anxious to have their sleds back. She gave him a saucy wink and slipped out from under him. "I guess you don't know me nearly as well as you think you do."

For the first time since he'd met her, Richard began to wonder if that might not be true. The possibility flat-out intrigued him.

They were still dusting snow from their clothes and bickering about the fairness of the race when they arrived at Anna Louise's.

She stood on the front porch gazing up at him. "Would you like a cup of coffee before you walk back? Or maybe some hot chocolate?"

"Put marshmallow on top of that chocolate and you have yourself a deal," he said, wondering when that sort of drink had become more appealing to him than a tumbler of aged Scotch whiskey. He realized that since he'd met Anna Louise only once had he needed the liquor to take the edge off of his memories. For that alone, he ought to be grateful.

It wasn't exactly gratitude he was feeling, though, as he sat across from her in front of a fire, sipping the sweet cocoa with its melting marshmallow topping. The fire lit her hair in a way that had him debating which red was brightest... or which was more dangerous. He felt a sudden yearning to run his fingers through the strands that wisped around her face and tumbled to her shoulders in careless, untended curls.

A stern reminder that she was off limits played through his head, but sounded weaker than usual. He settled for reaching into his pocket for the package of antique combs. He pulled it out and held it just out of her reach, deliberately forcing her to move closer to take it.

"You shouldn't have," she said, eyeing the small package speculatively.

He took it back. "If you don't want it..."

She scowled at him. "Hand it over."

"You are a greedy little thing."

"Just curious. I want to see what sort of taste you have," she said, taking the package and fingering it as if she wanted to guess its contents before opening it. Or maybe she just wanted to prolong the anticipation. That possibility delighted him in some inexplicable way, perhaps because it hinted that a gift from him might really matter to her.

Eventually, though, her patience wore thin and she ripped off the paper and opened the small, square box. At the sight of the silver combs, her eyes brightened with what just might have been the sheen of tears. "They're beautiful," she murmured, delicately tracing the silver.

He held out his hand. "May I put them in your hair?"

Her own hand trembled just a little as she held them out. Richard took the combs from the box. Scooping up a strand of her hair on one side, he held it in place with one comb, then followed the same pattern with the other. The light of the fire caught in her hair and glinted off the silver. His fingers remained tangled in her silken strands as his thumbs brushed against her cheeks, framing her face.

"You look so incredibly lovely," he whispered in a voice that had grown thick with emotion.

Anna Louise's eyes sparkled back at him. "Can I tell you something?"

"Anything."

"When I see the expression on your face, for the first time in my life I feel truly beautiful. Is it so terribly wicked to want to feel this way?"

"Never," he said as a sigh shuddered through him. He pulled her into his arms. "You are beautiful. Inside and out."

He could feel the rapid beat of her heart, the unmistakable quickening of her breath, and knew that they matched his own. It required every ounce of willpower he possessed to resist the temptation to do more than hold her close, to keep the promise he'd so recently made to himself.

"Richard?"

"Hmm?"

"Kiss me," she requested, her voice all soft vulnerability and sweetly innocent pleading.

He swallowed hard, his body aching with desire. The stern voice in his head protested, louder this time, but he pretended not to hear. One kiss. Was it so terribly much to ask? He had kissed her before, and it hadn't led to anything more.

Tonight, though? Something about tonight was magic, a continuation of the wondrous feelings first stirred in him during the Christmas Eve service. Could he deny himself, or her, on a night like tonight?

The answer came when he tilted her chin up and looked into her eyes, which were so filled with hope and longing. A heavier sigh shuddered through him.

"You do know how to test a man, Anna Louise," he murmured right before he settled his mouth over hers.

The feelings that rocked him then had less to do with raging desire than they did with something even more incredible, something even more alluring. For the first time since he'd returned to Kiley, Richard felt as if he'd truly come home.

After the holidays, Anna Louise started getting more harassing late-night calls filled with vitriolic accusations and dire threats. A woman's voice had been added to the man's now. Anonymous promises of eternal damnation became as commonplace as her bedtime prayers.

She refused to admit to anyone how shaken she was by the stepped-up intensity of the calls. In fact, she told no one they were happening. She should have known, though, that she couldn't keep them a secret forever.

"Looks like you have quite a few messages," Richard said one night after he'd brought her home from a visit with Maisey.

Anna Louise was in the kitchen fixing hot chocolate. The walks, the cocoa, the conversation and the sweetest, most wicked kisses she had ever known had become habit ever since Christmas night. It always stopped with kisses, though, as if Richard had set a line and nothing on earth or in heaven would get him to cross it.

"I'll listen to them later," she said just as he apparently pressed the play button.

With her heart climbing into her throat, she listened to the first message. It was innocuous enough.

Her youngest sister had called to ask how her holidays had been and to report that her brand new baby niece had loved the stuffed toy Anna Louise had sent.

Guessing that the simple words of her sister weren't all that was on that tape, she raced into the living room and tried to get to the machine before the next message could play. Richard apparently caught her panicked expression.

"What's wrong?" he asked at once.

"Nothing," she insisted, trying to stop the darn machine just as an all-too-familiar male voice began with its litany of Scripture. She was numb to the words, but with a sinking sensation in her heart, she watched the play of emotions on Richard's face—dismay, shock, outrage.

His gaze narrowed. "Who is that?"

"I don't know."

"What do you mean, you don't know? I can see from your expression that this guy has called before. He has, hasn't he? That's why you tore in here when I started the machine."

She nodded and tried to still the trembling of her hands. He sounded so angry.

"How often?" he demanded.

"More since Christmas."

"Who have you told?"

"No one."

He regarded her with astonishment. "Why the hell not?"

"I thought I could handle it. I've been dealing with people like this for years now."

"Is this what you call handling it? Letting some jerk terrify you?"

"It's not uncommon for a woman preacher to get calls like this. I've told you—"

"Right. There are people who don't approve of what you do. Why is that?" he asked furiously. "What the hell have you ever done to the people in this valley except treat them with kindness? Damn it, Anna Louise, why didn't you tell me about this?"

"I couldn't. I knew you'd react just the way you are."

"What did you expect? People like this ought to be strung up."

"That's no solution," she said stubbornly. "Given enough time, I can win them over. I know I can. And the ones I can't, well, they'd probably be happier over at Orville's church, anyway."

He rewound the tape and played it again...and again. "Does this sound like someone you can win over? The man is sick. He's not going to wake up one day and say, 'Gee whiz, that Anna Louise Perkins is a nice little lady, after all. I think I'll get off her case.'" He threw up his hands. "I don't know why any of this surprises me. It's typical of the small-mindedness around here."

"It is not," Anna Louise said adamantly, devastated that she'd been responsible for stirring up all of his old hatreds. "Most folks are not like this at all."

"I just don't get it. You are the kindest, most decent person I have ever met. If people can treat you like this, then I've been right all along, there is no good left in the world," he said bleakly.

"It's just one person," she argued, but he wouldn't listen. At least he hadn't heard the other voice. Maybe, given a day or two, she could persuade him to see reason.

"Why do you stay? You don't owe this town anything."

"I stay because I'm needed," she said simply. "And this is where I want to be. It's always better to stay and fight for what you believe in than it is to run, hoping to find someplace where things will be easier."

"I think you should call the sheriff, at least," he said.

"No."

"Anna Louise..."

"Richard, these aren't the first. They won't be the last. And I'm not the only woman pastor to be pestered this way. I seriously doubt if any of these people intend to act on their threats. They're just hoping to run me out of town. I'll face more of the same wherever I go. I've dared to break with tradition. There will always be people who can't handle that." She lifted her gaze to his. "Frankly, I'm not sure you can handle it."

He looked stunned by the accusation. "How can you possibly say that? Have I ever once suggested you don't belong in the ministry?"

"Maybe not," she agreed. "But I'll wager you wish I'd chosen a different profession."

He hesitated, clearly torn between honesty and admitting his own vulnerability.

"Maybe," he said finally. "But not for the reason you're thinking."

Anna Louise was elated that she'd steered him onto a subject she'd been trying to find a way to bring up for days. "How do you know what I'm thinking? I'm thinking if I weren't a preacher, you'd have made love to me by now."

An expression of shock spread across his face so quickly it was almost laughable. "Anna Louise," he protested.

"Well, it's true, isn't it?"

"I don't know."

"Liar."

"What are you asking me? Are you asking me to admit that I'm attracted to you? Hell, yes. I ache with it every time I get near you. You know damn well these chaste little kisses we've shared are sheer torment."

"But you've never done more than kiss me. Why is that?"

When he didn't answer, she offered her own interpretation, "Because I'm a preacher."

"It's not that simple, damn it."

"You're good with words. If that's not all there is to it, then explain it to me." She stood back and watched him struggle with himself over the explanation.

"You stand for something," he said finally. "Something I'm not sure I can believe in. I can't ask you to walk away from that and I'm not sure I can live with it."

"So you're saying there's no future for us, no chance at all because you can't accept what I do for a living. Isn't that exactly what I began by saying?"

"How the hell did we get away from this creep who's been calling you?" he said, running his hand through his hair in obvious exasperation.

"This is more important. Answer me."

"Okay," he said wearily. "The ministry is more than a career to you, Anna Louise. It's who you are. Your whole spirit is all about giving and decency. A part of me is drawn to that. Another part believes I'll just spoil it if I let you get too close to the reality I've experienced."

"Hogwash!"

He blinked and stared at her. "What?"

"Hogwash! You're just running scared. You don't want to acknowledge how much you want me because then you'd have to do something about it. Maybe you'd even have to make a commitment to something."

He backed off a step as if he feared she'd aggressively set out to seduce him if she could. "I will not sleep with you, Anna Louise."

"That's very noble."

"I will not allow you to taunt me into it."

She shrugged. "Who said I wanted to sleep with you?"

"Isn't that what this is all about?"

Heart thundering, she regarded him innocently. "I thought it was about those messages on my machine."

"Damn the messages. You and I have bigger problems to deal with."

She grinned. "I knew I could get your mind off those messages if I tried hard enough."

He studied her warily. "Is this some kind of game you've been playing the last few minutes?"

"Maybe. Maybe not."

He reached for her, then let his hands drop back by his sides. "I will not lose my temper," he muttered solemnly.

Anna Louise laughed out loud. "Do you honestly think your temper scares me?"

He scowled at her. "I'm not thinking about what effect it has on you. It scares the hell out of me. No one on earth infuriates me the way you do. You are the most annoying, most exasperating woman I have ever had the misfortune to be attracted to."

"Good."

"Good?" he repeated incredulously. "What the hell is good about it?"

"You're starting to feel again, Richard Walton. That's what's good about it. For a while now, I'd almost given up on you." She stood on tiptoe and planted a chaste little peck on his cheek. "Go home and think about that, why don't you."

Chapter Twelve

Richard had never been so furious or felt so helpless in his entire life. Not in Iraq. Not in Bosnia. Not in Haiti or Somalia. Maybe it was because those things had been beyond his power to control. But he should have been able to protect one incredibly special woman from the kind of harassment she was facing in supposedly safe and civilized Kiley, Virginia.

Over and over Richard heard those terrible messages playing in his head and wondered what kind of spiritual beliefs made excuses for hatred and harassment, especially when the target had brought only kindness and gentleness to everyone she met.

He tried telling himself it was not his fight. He tried to focus on the more pressing issue of what to do about the crazy turn Anna Louise's mind had unexpectedly taken. A few more kisses and wicked taunts and he wasn't going to be responsible for his actions.

As for that business about getting him to feel again, he supposed that was true enough. He just wasn't sure she was as ready as she thought she was to deal with what he was feeling. And he sure as hell wasn't ready to deal with the consequences of acting on those very same feelings. He'd suffered enough pangs of guilt in his time without actively courting more.

But as much as he tried to turn his attention away from those damnable messages and onto more provocative topics, he couldn't. He kept seeing Anna Louise's face as the terrible words had spilled from that tape. It wasn't fear he read in her eyes. It was anguish. She was deeply hurt that anyone could hate her so much.

It might be better if she got angry, he thought. The way he had. Fury led to action and that was what he believed with all his heart that she needed. This was no time to be turning the other cheek.

He broached the idea of discovering the caller's identity while sitting in her kitchen a few nights later. "I'll hire a private investigator," he suggested. "We'll nail this guy and put an end to it."

Anna Louise regarded him with a rueful expression. "This is Kiley. How long do you think a stranger would go unnoticed? He'd only drive the caller further underground."

"There are devices we could put on the phone, ways to trace the calls," he argued.

"Identifying him won't change the way he thinks. And there will always be someone else to take his place. I won't live like a victim. He's not out to harm me, just to drive me away."

Richard shook his head and lifted her hand to his lips. "I can't decide if you're incredibly brave or an idiot."

She smiled at him. "Neither one. I've just lived with this before. I've accepted that it comes with the territory."

"It's not right, damn it!"

"Nope," she agreed. "But no one knows better than you that life isn't always fair."

"Shouldn't your God protect you from this kind of antagonism?"

Her face paled slightly at his bitter sarcasm. "Maybe He's just trying to test my strength," she replied.

She said it so quietly and with such acceptance that Richard wanted to shake her. Seeing the stubborn lift of her chin, he heaved a sigh of resignation. "I wish I had half as much strength as you do."

"You do," she reassured him. "You've managed to resist me."

He couldn't help grinning at that. He supposed she had a point. As tests went, that was without question one of the toughest he'd ever faced. Nobody was more surprised than he was that he was passing.

Maybe he couldn't get Anna Louise to actively do something to identify her tormentor, but there was at least one thing he could do without bringing down her wrath. He could talk to Orville. If his old friend vocally opposed Anna Louise, then maybe he'd have some idea if one of his followers would take whatever he said and carry it to an extreme.

The next morning he went into the drugstore to see Tucker.

"Morning, Richard. What brings you out so early?" Tucker said, pouring him a cup of coffee before he could ask. "Care for a piece of coffee cake? It's fresh. Has a touch of raspberry preserves in the middle."

Richard grinned, despite his otherwise grim mood. "You know I can't resist raspberries." When he had the coffee cake in front of him and had taken his first bite, he inquired casually, "How's Orville getting along these days?"

"Haven't you seen him?"

"Only the day of the flood."

"To tell the truth, he sticks pretty close to home over in Jasper Junction most of the time these days. He knows I don't approve of this vendetta he has going with Anna Louise."

"He's trying to get her thrown out, isn't he?"

Tucker heaved a sigh of regret. "I'd say he'd have her tarred and feathered if he could. I don't know how that boy can call himself a man of God and be so intolerant."

"Does everyone know how he feels?"

"He doesn't make a secret of it, if that's what you're asking." Tucker's gaze narrowed. "What is it, Richard? Is somebody giving Anna Louise trouble?"

"She's had some calls. They're not from Orville. I'd have recognized his voice. I was thinking, though, that he might know who's responsible."

"I'll get him right over here," Tucker said, reaching for his phone, his expression as grim now as Richard's.

"Don't. I'll take a drive over to Jasper Junction. I want to catch him off guard."

Tucker nodded. "If there's anything I can do, let me know."

"Just don't tell Anna Louise I've been asking questions. She's determined to handle this herself and she won't thank me for interfering."

"Then you'd better get a move on. She'll be by for her morning coffee any minute now."

Richard reached for his wallet, but Tucker waved off the money. "It's on the house. Just go give that son of mine what-for."

Richard found Orville in the parsonage over in Jasper Junction. His welcoming smile faded at once, when he caught Richard's sober expression.

"What is it? Maisey's okay, isn't she?"

Richard nodded, studying his old friend. Orville might be a preacher like Anna Louise, but he didn't have her aura of serenity about him. If anything, he looked uptight as the dickens. Feeling guilty, maybe.

"I wanted to talk to you about Anna Louise," he said.

Orville's expression changed, instantly became wary. "I heard you've been spending time with her."

"That's not the point. Someone's harassing her. He claims to have a direct line from God telling him she has no business being in the profession she's chosen."

"She doesn't," Orville said curtly. "If you'd like to take a look at the Bible, I can show you the exact passages—"

"I don't want to see the Scripture. I've heard enough of it from this caller. You have your point of view. She has hers. I don't even want to say who's right, because I have no idea. I just know that Anna Louise doesn't deserve to be tormented this way, not by anyone. It's certainly not the charitable behavior I'd expect from one claiming such lofty ties."

His gaze pinned Orville. "I don't suppose you'd be egging this person on?"

"I would never deliberately do that," his old friend said, though his voice lacked a certain amount of convincing indignation.

"And if you discovered who did, you'd set 'em straight, wouldn't you?"

"You know I would."

Richard shook his head. "Sorry. I'm not so sure about anything where you're concerned. Just do what you can to see that this stops."

Orville nodded. "If the opportunity arises, I surely will."

Even though the words came from a preacher's lips, Richard didn't quite believe him. That made him sorrier than he could say.

*   *   *

As Richard struggled with his conscience and his heart, knowing that the day was coming when he could no longer remain detached and uninvolved, his grandmother took a turn for the worse. He came back from a long, quiet walk to find her short of breath and having chest pains.

"I'm taking you to the hospital," he said at once.

"Just call the doctor."

"Not this time."

"Please," she said, clinging to his hand. "If it's my time, I want to die here."

Richard's heart began to thud dully as he contemplated the matter-of-fact statement and its terrible implications. Still, he couldn't go against her wishes. In her own way, Maisey was every bit as strong-willed as Anna Louise. Maybe Doc Benson would have better luck persuading her that her chances were better in an intensive care unit.

"I'll get the doctor over here right away," he said, terrified by the prospect of leaving her side even long enough to make the call. "I'll be right back. Will you be okay?"

"You're only going to the parlor," she said, forcing a smile.

He made the call, listened anxiously to the endless ringing and very nearly panicked. "Where the hell have you been?" he snapped when Jonathan Benson finally answered.

"Coming back from delivering a baby," he said quietly. "Is it Maisey?"

"She's having a lot of pain and she can't catch her breath."

"And she won't let you take her to the hospital," the doctor guessed. "I'm on my way. I'll call for an ambulance."

"She says she won't go."

"She'll go this time if I have to knock her out," Benson vowed so heatedly that Richard had to grin.

"I take it you've had this discussion before."

"Endlessly. I'm on my way."

An hour later Richard was in the back of the ambulance as it raced toward Charlottesville. Maisey glared at him the entire trip. He tried to tell himself it was a good sign, but all he could think about was how cold and frail her hand felt in his.

"I want to see Anna Louise," she said as they roared into the emergency entrance.

Richard regarded her worriedly. "You're going to be okay. Didn't you hear Doc Benson tell you that?"

"I want to see her," she insisted.

His heart thumping unsteadily, he nodded. "I'll call the minute we get there." He couldn't bring himself to admit how badly he wanted Anna Louise there, as well, how much he had come to depend on her commonsense approach, on her laughter, on her quiet strength.

Maisey's admission was a blur. All he remembered was Doc Benson muttering reassurances as they wheeled her from view. A nurse directed him to a waiting room outside Cardiac Intensive Care, told him where he could find coffee and left him to his frantic thoughts.

He tried to sit and couldn't. He paced. And cursed. And, finally, he prayed. It was all he could think of to do. Whether his prayers for Maisey were heard, he had no way of knowing, but Anna Louise did appear by his side just when he thought he'd go crazy from the waiting.

"How is she?" she asked, slipping her hand into his and leading him to a chair.

"They haven't said a damn thing since we got here. They have this drug now that's supposed to burst clots, if it's given soon enough. I read about it. Doc Benson didn't say anything about a bypass. Do you suppose she has the strength to survive surgery?"

"I think that you're making yourself nuts with all of this speculating. Let me go see what I can find out."

"They won't let you in."

"Yes, they will," she said confidently. "I'm a preacher. They won't deny me the right to be with her."

As grateful as he was that at least someone dear to Maisey would be with her, Richard couldn't bear the thought that the only reason Anna Louise might be admitted was because his grandmother was dying.

Anna Louise's spirits sank at the sight of Maisey looking so incredibly pale against the white sheets, hooked up to tubes and monitors. She had paid visits to hundreds of patients, comforted their families, but never before with this terrible sense of personal loss crowding her thoughts.

Maisey appeared to be sleeping. Doc Benson was nowhere in sight, but as she'd expected, the nurses had given their approval for Anna Louise to sit with Maisey for a while. She pulled up a chair and took Maisey's hand in her own. She wasn't aware she was crying until a tear splashed against her fingers.

Apparently Maisey felt it, as well, because she opened her eyes. "Anna Louise, you're here," she said weakly. "I'm so glad. Just don't go drowning me with those tears."

"I wouldn't be anywhere else. Stop talking now and rest."

"Richard?"

"He's in the waiting room."

"Is he okay?"

"He's worried about you."

Maisey dampened her lips and seemed to be struggling to catch her breath. Anna Louise smoothed a hand over her forehead. "Ssh. Don't try to talk."

"Have to," Maisey insisted. "Worried."

"Please don't worry about anything. Just concentrate on getting well."

"No. If it's my time, I'm ready to go. Richard will have a terrible time with that. Please, promise me."

"Promise you what?"

"That you won't let him blame himself."

"Why would he do that?"

"For not coming home sooner. He's always taken everything so personally. His parents' deaths, all the world's problems. He thinks he should be able to change things. You and I know it doesn't work that way. Help him to see that. Promise.''

Anna Louise drew in a deep breath at the difficult task Maisey had set for her. The past weeks had taught her that even with all of her faith she might not be up to changing his way of thinking. But for Maisey's sake and, more importantly, for Richard's, she would try.

''I promise,'' she said softly.

Maisey managed a faint smile and squeezed her hand, then closed her eyes and drifted back to sleep.

Before she left the cardiac unit, Anna Louise asked one of the nurses to track down Jonathan Benson. She gazed into his troubled brown eyes and forced herself to ask, ''Will she make it?''

''There's always a chance,'' he said. ''But I'd say she could use your prayers. They'll do as much for her now as I can.''

Her spirits low, she forced herself to go back to the waiting room. Richard took one look at her expression and sank into a chair and put his face in his hands.

When he finally lifted his head and met her gaze, he said, ''It's bad, isn't it?'' He sounded numb.

''I believe she can pull through this,'' Anna Louise said adamantly. She knelt down in front of him and took his face in her hands. ''We have to pray for that.''

''But—''

She refused to hear his arguments. ''No, *both* of us. Please, Richard. For Maisey's sake.'' Without giving him a chance to protest, she began a familiar prayer, repeating the words slowly and quietly, listening desperately for the sound of Richard's voice joining hers. Finally she heard the first halting words. By the time she said *Amen*, his voice was stronger. It might not have held conviction, but she was almost positive she heard hope.

It was a start.

The night seemed endless to Richard. Anna Louise slept curled up in a chair. He'd found a blanket to put over her. He knew it was selfish of him to let her stay on, but he couldn't bear to face whatever was ahead alone.

They had let him see Maisey twice and each time for only a few minutes. Even after years of reporting from terrible make-shift hospitals in war zones, nothing had prepared him for the shock of seeing her like that. Each time he had left the cardiac intensive care unit, he had prayed a little harder. Not because he believed it did any good, but because he could think of nothing else to do.

It was dawn when Doc Benson came into the waiting room. Anna Louise apparently heard his voice and woke up. She stood up and moved closer to Richard's side, as if willing him to feel her strength.

"I think she could pull through," the doctor said with cautious optimism.

"Are you sure?" Richard said, not daring to believe it was possible.

"There are no certainties," the doctor warned. "But she seems a little stronger this morning. The medicine has regulated her heartbeat. Her color is better. She's asking to see you both.''

"Can we go in?"

"Give the nurses a few minutes to finish up their shift—change reports, then go on in. Just don't stay too long.''

"Thank you for staying the night," Richard said. "Not many doctors would have done that.''

"That's why I chose to practice in a place like Kiley. It allows me to be where I'm needed. I'm going home for a shower and a change of clothes now. I'll see you both later.''

When he was gone, Richard drew Anna Louise into his arms. "She's going to make it. I believe that now with all my heart.''

"Our prayers were answered," she said with absolute conviction.

Richard couldn't help but wonder if this time, anyway, she might be right. Perhaps God had heard the prayers of one wayward, lonely reporter, after all. Or maybe having someone who believed as strongly as Anna Louise did by his side had made all the difference.

"How did your faith get to be so strong?" he asked for the second time in recent days, still unclear about what drove her to be so open to other people's needs and demands in the face of their sometimes thankless responses. "Why did you choose such a difficult path?"

"It was no choice, at all. It was what I had to do," she said with quiet simplicity.

The answer brought him no real satisfaction. He needed something specific that would help him to understand the woman who had come to mean more and more to him with each day that passed. At his prodding, she finally tried to elaborate.

"I felt I had a calling to share my faith with others. I believed I was living proof that miracles can happen and I had an obligation to repay that miracle that God granted me by letting me live against all the odds."

"Wasn't there another way you could have demonstrated your gratitude?"

"You're accusing me of being ambitious, of not knowing my place."

Richard shook his head. "I'm not accusing you of anything. I'm just trying to understand you."

"Why?"

"Because..." His words faltered. "Because you matter to Maisey," he said finally, because he wasn't ready to admit just how much she had come to mean to him. If he admitted what he knew in his heart was true—that he was falling in love with her—then he'd have to find a way to reconcile his life-style and hers. He wasn't ready to do that just yet.

What he was ready to admit was that he wanted to find the same kind of peace inside himself that radiated from her, that he was almost ready to stop running from a past that had eaten at him every day of the past nine years.

While they waited out the minutes until they could go to see Maisey, Richard held Anna Louise in his arms, drawing comfort from her nearness. He wondered as that increasingly familiar contentment stole through him, if he wasn't starting to experience that miracle Anna Louise believed in, after all.

He heard her sharp intake of breath, then felt her pulling away.

"What is it?" he asked, looking down into her troubled eyes.

"Millicent," she said curtly, nodding toward the open doorway.

"Millicent Rawlings? Why is that so terrible? She's probably heard about Maisey and come to check on her."

"And found me in your arms."

"Is comforting a member of your flock off limits?"

"That won't be the interpretation she puts on it," Anna Louise said.

Richard heard the genuine concern in her voice. He wanted to contradict her, but he, better than anyone, knew the likelihood that she was right.

One thing at a time, he warned himself. See that Maisey got well and then he could take on all the people of Kiley, if he had to, to see that Anna Louise's happiness there was assured.

Chapter Thirteen

Millicent Rawlings had a lot to say to Anna Louise, all in the guise of gentle advice, of course. She had dressed for the occasion in a puritanical black dress, a black felt hat with a feather in it and a black winter coat. If Anna Louise hadn't known better, she would have thought someone in town had died.

"I do hate to bring this up, Anna Louise," she began with a prim little smile that didn't show much evidence of regret. If anything, she looked suspiciously gleeful.

Anna Louise braced herself. She had seen Millicent's startled expression when she had spotted Anna Louise in Richard's arms outside Maisey's hospital room the day before. She'd been expecting a confrontation ever since, despite Richard's reassurances that there was nothing to be upset about. Finding Millicent on her doorstep at 9:00 a.m. hadn't surprised Anna Louise in the slightest. If anything, she'd expected her sooner.

"What is it, Millicent?"

The older woman pushed past her, oblivious to the fact that Anna Louise hadn't invited her inside. "Well, I'm not one to gossip..." She paused expectantly.

"No, of course not," Anna Louise said dutifully.

"It's just that you have been spending a great deal of time lately with a certain young man..."

"Richard Walton," Anna Louise supplied helpfully, determined to hang on to her temper as long as she possibly could. Unfortunately, it was already simmering. And Millicent's coy approach to the issue wasn't helping. Why couldn't she just say whatever was on her mind and be done with it? "That is who you mean, isn't it?"

"Yes. Richard Walton," she said grimly.

Millicent drew herself up until she reminded Anna Louise of a puffed-up, self-important hen.

"This has been a matter of concern for some time now, but after yesterday morning, well, I just knew the time had come when I had to say something."

"What happened yesterday morning?" Anna Louise inquired. A saint couldn't have sounded more innocent, she decided proudly.

"It was what I saw with my own eyes at the hospital. I can't begin to tell you how upsetting I found it."

"What exactly do you think you saw?" Anna Louise asked coldly, finally recognizing that she was going to have to pry every word out of the woman.

This time apparently Millicent heard the warning note in her voice. She regarded Anna Louise closely. "Why, I saw you in that man's arms, right out where all the world could see you. With Maisey Walton on her deathbed not more than a few feet away. I have to admit I was stunned that you would pick such a time to engage in something like *that*," she said, giving the word an emphasis that managed to make it sound like Anna Louise and Richard had been making love in plain view. She paused and studied Anna Louise thoughtfully. "Perhaps you, being an outsider and all..."

"I've lived here for five years," Anna Louise reminded her, then recalled that the people of Kiley had treated Janie Walton as an outsider even after she'd been there for fifteen years.

"That's not very long in a town like Kiley," Millicent said as if she'd read her mind. "And you are in a unique position, one that should be above reproach."

Anna Louise leveled her gaze straight at Millicent. "Exactly what is it you think I've done?" She wanted Millicent to be very clear about what she was accusing her of doing. That was the only way to nip such irresponsible gossip in the bud. Thank heavens, the woman had come straight to her, rather than talking about what she'd seen with every single person in town except the supposedly guilty parties. Millicent would save her gossip for after this encounter.

"I'm not saying you've *done* anything," Millicent reassured her quickly. "It's just that appearances are so important in a small town, especially for a pastor."

"I certainly agree, but what is your point?"

"You know we all love Maisey..." Another of those expectant pauses.

When she could see that Millicent actually expected a response, Anna Louise nodded. "Of course."

"Maisey is a treasure, but even those of us who try to be charitable have to admit that that grandson of hers is another kettle of fish entirely."

"You have a problem with Richard?"

Millicent apparently missed Anna Louise's deadly tone. "They say genes do tell, don't they?"

Anna Louise tucked her hands firmly under her and sat perfectly still. The temptation to smack the woman was almost irresistible. For a woman who claimed not to be a gossip, Millicent certainly had a very long memory. "Meaning?" she said, as if she had no idea what Millicent was driving at.

"Well, his mother. Of course, you wouldn't know about that. It was a long time ago and we don't talk about it much, in deference to Maisey."

Anna Louise was about one breath away from exploding. She was beginning to see why the people of Kiley set Richard's teeth on edge. "If it was all so long ago and something that's no longer discussed, then I'm afraid I don't see your point and I really have things I need to be doing."

Millicent wasn't about to be shut up now. She was clearly on a mission and she intended to see it through.

She drew herself up. "Okay, then, let me be blunt. Don't you think there's something a little unusual about Richard Walton?"

Anna Louise regarded her blankly. "Unusual? In what way precisely?"

"You know." She actually looked around as if he might be listening nearby, then said in a whisper, "Dangerous."

Anna Louise's expression turned deliberately thoughtful. That certainly described Richard, all right, though she doubted she and Millicent put precisely the same definition to the word. Still, regardless of the interpretation, she didn't think she ought to be conceding a thing to Millicent.

"Dangerous?" she said with a puzzled frown. "No, I don't believe I had noticed that."

"Well, it's something to consider, don't you think? Especially for a woman in your position. You can't afford to be too careful about those with whom you choose to associate."

It required all of Anna Louise's self-restraint to keep from telling Millicent to mind her own blasted business. After drawing in a deep breath, she managed to say calmly, "In my position, I'm supposed to be responsible for the souls of the sinners as well as the saints. As a matter of fact, if what you say is true, Richard probably needs me more than some others, don't you think?"

The carefully posed question seemed to catch her parishioner off guard.

"Well, yes, I suppose I can see how you would need to give him a certain amount of attention," she admitted with obvious reluctance.

"I was sure you would," Anna Louise said dryly.

"But you were in his *arms,* Anna Louise. Surely you can see how that might be misinterpreted."

"Only by someone who was small-minded, though, don't you agree?" she said sweetly. "After all, the man was clearly worried sick about his grandmother. Surely, anyone would have offered a little comfort."

Unfortunately, before Millicent had time to digest Anna Louise's lesson in equal opportunity salvation and her implication that Millicent had a dirty, narrow mind, the man in question walked onto the porch, rapped on the door and strolled inside. To an outsider it would definitely look as if he felt a little too much at home. It probably wouldn't matter, given the current conversation, that almost everyone in Kiley strolled through unlocked doors in much the same way.

"Richard, I'm so glad you found the time to stop by and fix the..." She stumbled over the fabricated excuse for his untimely presence. If she let on what Millicent was there about, all the diversionary tactics in the world wouldn't keep Richard's temper from going straight through the roof. She was determined to avoid that at all costs.

His brow knit in a puzzled frown. "Fix what?"

"The faucet," she said, latching on to the first thing that came to mind.

He stared at her blankly. "Your faucet's leaking? Why didn't you—"

"Thank you for coming so quickly," she said, regarding him pointedly. "I know you need to be getting to the hospital to visit Maisey, but that drip really has been driving me crazy. It'll be a relief to see it fixed."

Apparently she finally got through his thick skull. He nodded slowly. "Right. The faucet. I'll get my tools and see what I can do."

Only then did he direct his gaze toward Millicent, who was sitting stiffly on the edge of her chair, her mouth turned down in a disapproving frown. "Morning, Millicent. You're looking particularly fetching this morning. New dress?"

Anna Louise watched with amusement as Millicent struggled against being pleased by the flattery.

"Thank you, young man," she said finally. "Don't you think you should be getting those tools now?"

"Sure," he said easily, and left Anna Louise alone with Millicent.

"You needn't stay," Anna Louise told her. "I'm sure you have a million things to do. Didn't I hear you were organizing a group to play bridge at the new recreation hall now that it's finished?"

Millicent's jaw set stubbornly. "Well, of course I'm staying. I will not leave you alone in this house with *him*. Whatever would people say? The bridge club will just have to wait."

Anna Louise lost patience. "People won't say anything about Richard dropping by to do me a favor, if you don't stir them up by reporting it to everyone you see."

Millicent looked taken aback by the sharp tone and the suggestion that she was a gossip. "I'm just thinking of your reputation, dear," she protested.

"And I appreciate your concern. I really do. But let me worry about my reputation, okay? If I'm uncertain of the right path, I'll pray for guidance."

The older woman couldn't seem to come up with an argument to counter that. Even Millicent would have to concede that God was a higher authority. "Well, if you're absolutely sure you don't want me to stay," she murmured with obvious regret.

"Really, it's not the least bit necessary," Anna Louise reassured her cheerfully. "Richard will be finished and on his way to see Maisey before you know it."

Millicent took her own dear sweet time about getting to the door. She lingered long enough to see that Richard did indeed have his tools with him when he came back up the walk.

"You give your grandmother my love," she told him briskly.

"I'll do that, Millicent. I know she appreciated your coming by yesterday, even if you weren't allowed in to see her."

"Well, you tell her I'll be back again the minute she's up to having visitors." She gave Anna Louise a significant look. "Now you be real careful, dear. Remember what I told you."

Anna Louise sighed. "I'm not likely to forget it, Millicent."

As soon as Millicent had strolled off toward town, Anna Louise muttered a curse that had Richard staring at her in openmouthed astonishment. "Oh, don't look at me like that," she snapped. "That woman is infuriating."

"What was she doing here, anyway?"

"She stopped by to give me a little friendly advice."

He regarded her warily. "About what?"

"You, of course."

"So that's why I'm toting these tools around."

"Well, I had to say something. She was about to turn that embrace she caught us in at the hospital yesterday into a rip-roaring affair. My reputation would have been mud by dusk, especially with you turning up here first thing this morning."

He studied her thoughtfully. "Are you really worried about what Millicent Rawlings could do to your reputation? Everybody knows she's an old busybody."

Anna Louise didn't like the way he was dismissing the incident so casually. He certainly ought to understand how easy it was to become an outcast in Kiley thanks to unfounded gossip. "To hear her tell it, you're no better than your mother," she said, just to prove this was no laughing matter.

The amusement in his eyes vanished in a heartbeat, replaced by quick anger. "I should have known, damn it. How dare she? By Heaven, I will rip that sorry tongue of hers right out of her throat."

"That will certainly quiet the talk," Anna Louise noted.

He glared at her. "Okay, you're right. There's no point in stirring things up." His gaze narrowed. "You're not really upset about this, are you? If one word of this spreads beyond Millicent, I promise you I'll deal with it."

"It's just more ammunition for my opponents, if they get wind of it," she said wearily. "I guarantee they'll use any evidence of misconduct on my part to bolster their cause to be rid of me."

"That's absurd. You haven't done anything. Hell, *we*, haven't done anything."

Suddenly Anna Louise saw the irony in the situation. She started to chuckle, which was a stark contrast to Richard's thoroughly sober expression.

"Now what's so damn funny?" he asked.

"I'm about to be labeled some sort of Jezebel and I can't even get you to do anything more than kiss me," she said. "If I'm going to have the reputation, I'd at least like the fun of earning it."

He shook his head, tolerant amusement written all over his face. "No, you wouldn't, sweetheart. You only get to be really angry and self-righteous when you're innocent of all charges. I think that's what kept my mother from fighting back. Billy Joe had one tiny nugget of truth mixed in with all the innuendo. It was enough to keep her silent."

She scowled at him. "I hate it when you make perfect sense."

"I know."

He plopped his tools in the middle of her foyer and held out his hand. She regarded it with far more wariness than Adam had probably displayed when Eve held out that apple in the Garden of Eden. "What's that for?"

"I was just going to take your hand. Almost nobody makes an issue of two people holding hands in public."

She stuffed both hands in her pockets. "Millicent would."

"Does that mean you don't even want to be seen riding through town with me?"

"Riding? Where?"

"Did you forget why I came over here this morning? We're supposed to go see Maisey."

She gave him a rueful smile. "I suppose I had or I would have told Millicent that in the first place." She glanced at his out-held hand. "Maybe I was just engaging in a little wishful thinking."

"Oh?"

"For a minute there, maybe I was hoping Millicent had been right about your low-down, sneaky intentions."

"Has anybody ever mentioned that for a preacher, you have an incredibly active and misdirected imagination?"

"Fortunately, you're the only one in town who knows that and you're not inclined to take advantage of it," she said bleakly. "Let's go see Maisey."

All the way to Charlottesville, Richard kept sneaking glances at Anna Louise. She seemed oddly put-out with him for some reason. He wasn't sure if she blamed him for the embrace that had stirred Millicent Rawlings up or if she blamed him for not taking advantage of her. Maybe he should have admitted one more time exactly how she tested his willpower.

"Anna Louise?"

"Yes."

"You're not mad, are you?"

"Mad about what?"

He regarded her with exasperation. "That's what I'm trying to find out."

"No, I'm not angry," she said in a tone that conveyed exactly the opposite impression.

Richard fell silent. They were about three miles from a rest area where he could pull off the road and do something about this funk she was in. When he turned into the little roadside park, she regarded him with obvious confusion.

"What's wrong? Why are we stopping?"

Richard didn't say a word. He pulled into a space, cut the engine, then slowly turned to face her.

"What?" she said, apparently alerted by something in his expression.

"Come here."

"Richard, what has gotten into you?"

"The same thing that has gotten into me from the day I found you in Maisey's orchard. *You,* my sweet, innocent little preacher, have gotten into me."

Her eyes widened. She glanced around hurriedly, taking in the fact that there were no other cars parked in the rest area. "I'm not sure . . ."

"Not sure of what? Not sure that this is such a good idea? Neither am I," he said grimly. "But I will not have you thinking for one single instant that you are not the most desirable, outrageously sexy woman on the face of the earth or that I don't want you."

A spark of heat flared in her eyes, warming the color to the exact shade of brandy. Her mouth slowly curved into a smile. "Honest?"

Richard's entire body ached with longing. "That's the truth, Anna Louise. I think it would be a mistake, but I will prove it, if that's what you want."

She glanced around the cramped interior of the compact car. "Here?" she said doubtfully.

He grinned. "It's not the spot I would have chosen, but anything is possible if you're desperate enough."

She regarded him intently. "Are you desperate enough?"

He took the question seriously, not because her tone said it was, but because he read the need in her eyes. "A day or night has not gone by in the past few weeks when I haven't thought about making love to you, about what your skin would feel like, about how you would taste, about how you would look when you came apart in my arms."

With his gaze pinned on Anna Louise, he saw that she was swallowing hard, as caught up in the fantasy as he was.

"I have a list about a mile long of all the reasons we shouldn't do anything," he told her. "I go over it instead of counting sheep. Unfortunately, instead of putting me to sleep, it keeps me wide awake and thoroughly aroused. Every single one of those reasons is valid, but I will toss them all out the window if you are absolutely certain that making love with me is what you want."

She frowned. "That doesn't sound very romantic. It sounds more like a business proposition."

Richard gripped the steering wheel so tightly that his knuckles turned white. It was the only way he could keep from reaching for her. "Sweetheart, getting carried away by passion is the easiest thing in the world. Believe me, I know. But making a decision that is right, making a choice for all the right reasons, that takes something more. It takes something you deserve to have—unconditional love."

She sighed softly. Tears glistened in her eyes. "And you don't love me," she said flatly, trying her darnedest to sound brave.

Richard raked a hand through his hair. Now he'd done it. He'd gotten into something he'd never intended. He absolutely could not tell her that he did indeed love her and then follow that up by saying that when the time came he would leave, anyway.

"I care about you," he said cautiously. "Enough not to do anything you'd wind up regretting."

Anna Louise turned her head away.

"Look at me," he insisted. "Please."

Slowly she turned back. Tears were tracking down her cheeks. The sight of them made his heart ache. He reached over and brushed away the tears with the tips of his fingers. "Don't cry, sweetheart. Please don't cry."

"Richard Walton, if you weren't just about the nicest, most honorable man in the entire universe, I think I'd slug you," she said, her voice choked.

A sigh shuddered through Richard then. She would be okay, he reassured himself. Anna Louise might be a preacher, but she was also a hellion. Nothing would get her down for long, not even watching him walk out of her life.

Too bad he couldn't hold out the same high hopes for himself. He had a feeling that leaving Anna Louise behind, no matter how firmly he believed that it was the right thing—the *only* thing—to do, was going to cost him dearly. In fact, he wondered if he'd ever find a way to recover from the loss.

Chapter Fourteen

"What kept you two?" Maisey demanded the minute Anna Louise and Richard walked into the intensive care unit. She was still being monitored by a lot of equipment, but she was sitting up and looking considerably more chipper than she had when she'd been admitted.

Before either of them could respond, she peered more closely at Anna Louise. "You've been crying." She scowled at Richard. "What did you do to her?"

"It's nothing," Anna Louise said hurriedly before Richard's conscience demanded that he make a full confession on the spot. She wasn't ready to talk about her feelings for Richard or his lack of feelings for her just yet, not even with the one person on the face of the earth who would understand how complex the situation was.

Trying to redirect Maisey's attention, Anna Louise asked cheerfully, "How are you today? You look much better."

"That's because they're pumping me full of drugs," Maisey said dryly. "Puts a nice fuzzy glow around everything." Her expression sobered. "I don't like it. How's a person supposed to know how she really feels? I told Doc Benson they've given me my last shot of this stuff. I'd rather have a little pain every now and again."

"And what did he say?" Anna Louise asked, envisioning that particular confrontation with some amusement.

"He told me he was the one with the medical degree and I'd do what he said," Maisey said, practically shaking with indignation. "Can you imagine the nerve of that young man?"

Richard grinned. "I think I'm liking this doctor better and better."

"Don't go getting any ideas based on the way he treats me," Maisey warned him. "He might be able to pull rank, but you can't. In fact, I think you and I need to have a little talk."

"When you're out of here," he said agreeably.

"I don't think so. Now. Anna Louise, will you excuse us for a minute?"

"No," she said, and pulled up a chair to emphasize the point.

Maisey looked startled by her open rebellion. "Why not?"

"Because you're supposed to be recuperating, not meddling."

"I'd rest a lot easier if I knew things between you two were on track. I might be a little fuzzy-headed this morning, but I'm not blind. Something's wrong."

Anna Louise felt tears welling up in her eyes again. If this kept up she was going to start blubbering for the second time in a single morning. "Richard and I are adults, Maisey. We are capable of handling our own lives."

"That's right," Richard echoed.

"Fiddle-faddle. If you were, you'd have a wedding date set by now."

At that, Anna Louise's tears began to flow again in earnest. She ran out of the room. As the door closed behind her, she heard Richard say, "Now look what you've done."

To which Maisey replied, "Sounds to me like the pot calling the kettle black. No woman cries at the mention of a wedding, unless some man has recently disappointed her. When are you going to wake up and smell the coffee? If you wait till you're even half my age, you'll have lost the best woman you're ever likely to meet."

Anna Louise didn't hear what Richard said to that. She headed for a ladies' room, where she could finish up her cry in peace, then repair the damage to her makeup before going back to face Maisey and her exasperating, noble grandson.

Locking herself in one of the stalls, she allowed the tears to fall for another couple of minutes before determinedly drying her eyes. If the man couldn't admit that he loved her, if he couldn't make the kind of commitment it took to make a marriage work, then it was his loss. She felt sorry for him. She would pray that someday he would find the courage to build a life with someone who loved him half as much as she did, someone who would lift him out of the depressions his work generated.

In the meantime she would never again let him see her shed another tear over him. She would make no demands. She'd be so pleasant and lukewarm in her attitude toward him that he couldn't possibly feel threatened. If he wanted to go through life in neutral, then she was not going to waste another instant fighting him.

Feeling stronger and more determined, she finally let herself out of the stall and washed her face. She powdered her nose and touched up her lipstick. She was even able to convince herself that there was no more evidence of the tears she'd shed. She accomplished that by not looking into the mirror for more than the split second it took to fix her makeup.

Unfortunately, all of her good intentions seemed to have been wasted. When she walked back into the intensive care unit, she found Richard's grandmother alone. Judging from the determined expression on Maisey's face, Anna Louise wasn't going to get out of there without answering every single question on her mind.

She considered bolting, then decided that would only postpone the inevitable. "Where's Richard?"

"I sent him to get me a magazine."

"Maisey, I left you with a stack of magazines yesterday."

"He doesn't know that."

Anna Louise resigned herself. She sat back down by Maisey's side. "Okay. What's on your mind?"

"You and that grandson of mine. It's plain as day to me how the two of you feel about each other. What's the holdup?"

If she hadn't been so exhausted by the whole situation, Anna Louise might have found Maisey's divide-and-conquer routine amusing. "I think your illness has made your vision a little fuzzy," she told her. "It's probably those drugs you mentioned. I mean absolutely nothing to Richard."

"Fiddle-faddle," Maisey said emphatically. "Can't you see the way he looks at you?"

"What way is that?" she inquired, trying to keep the fascinated note from her voice. She was downright pitiful. She was relying on a woman in intensive care to tell her things she should have been able to figure out herself. And she was doing it not five minutes after she'd sworn to walk away from him without a backward glance.

"Oh, for goodness' sakes, girl, the man is crazy in love with you."

Anna Louise nodded slowly. "I knew it," she murmured, grateful to have her own guesswork confirmed even if it meant nothing in the long run.

"What's that?" Maisey said.

Apparently her hearing was sharper than her vision, Anna Louise thought ruefully. "I said you were imagining things."

Maisey waved off the criticism. "Don't tell me I don't know my own grandson. As for you, you look just as lovesick as he does. Worse, maybe."

That was hardly a comfort. "Maisey, I appreciate your concern, but I will not discuss this with you. It's too upsetting."

"For me or for you?" Maisey inquired pointedly.

Anna Louise leveled a stubborn look straight at her. "Not another word on this subject or I'm out of here."

"Oh, for heaven's sake," Maisey protested, then sighed. "Okay, whatever you say."

Anna Louise started to sit back and relax, prepared to have a nice, quiet visit during the remaining time she was allowed to stay. It didn't last.

"The vote is coming soon, isn't it?" Maisey asked.

Anna Louise couldn't pretend she didn't know which vote Maisey had in mind. It was clear she was referring to the local church association's upcoming ballot on whether Anna Louise had the right to stay on as pastor of her church in Kiley. Orville had been threatening to make it an issue for months now and the time was fast approaching when the other area pastors would be forced to take a stand. If anything, Maisey looked even more worried about this than she had over whatever was going on between Richard and Anna Louise.

Anna Louise squeezed her hand. "Don't you worry about it. Everything's going to be okay. You just concentrate on getting well."

"We both know I'm not going to get well, not this time. I want to know you're going to be okay before I die. You deserve to stay on at the church. Those preachers have no right to take it away from you, if you're the pastor we want."

Anna Louise sighed. "Unfortunately, they do have the right. That's the way the church is structured. But I'm not going to go without a fight. I promise you that."

When she and Richard eventually left Maisey's hospital room, Anna Louise knew what she had to do. She'd put it off for too long now. She should have confronted Orville Patterson face-to-face months ago.

The minute Richard had dropped her off, she picked up the most recent message tape from her answering machine, one she hadn't erased. Then she got into her own car and headed straight for Jasper Junction.

She found Orville in a meeting with some of the church elders. The men exchanged looks that might have been amusing if they hadn't been so telling about their attitudes toward her.

"I doubt the roof will cave in, just because I've walked through the door," she said dryly. "Orville, I need to see you."

"I'm in the middle of a meeting. Can't we do it some other time?"

"I don't think this can wait. If you don't care to leave your associates here, I'd be happy to have this conversation in front of them."

The three men seemed to brighten a little at the prospect of a good fight, but Orville stood and said stiffly, "Follow me. We'll talk in my office. Excuse me, gentlemen. This won't take long."

In his office, Orville placed himself squarely behind his desk, leaned back in his swivel chair and regarded her with the smug look of a benevolent dictator. "Ready to throw in the towel, Miss Perkins?"

"Not a chance," she said adamantly. "But I am wondering if you might not want to reconsider your position."

"And just why would I do that? You know I am on solid ground in opposing you."

"I know no such thing," she shot back. "I'd like you to listen to something, though."

With obvious wariness, he studied the tape player she plunked on his desk. "What's that?"

"Surely, you've seen a tape player before," she said blithely. "This is just smaller than most."

"Of course. Really, Miss Perkins, I do not have time for this nonsense."

Anna Louise had grown tired of the insulting refusal to address her with her well-earned title. "It's *Pastor Perkins* and I think you'd better make the time," she said, hitting the play button.

This message was no worse than the others, but it was enough to turn Orville's expression ashen. "Billy Joe," he murmured.

Now it was Anna Louise's turn to gape. "Billy Joe Hunt? You recognize the voice?" Even though Orville didn't reply, by listening carefully, she could tell that he was right. It was Billy Joe Hunt. Dear Heaven, if Richard ever found out, he'd string the man up in the town square. Why on earth had he agreed to help build the recreation hall? That was something she'd have to ponder later.

"Do his arguments sound at all familiar?" she inquired.

"Well, I...." Orville sucked in a breath, his expression clearly shaken. "I suppose it's possible that someone could take what I've said and twist it, but I never intended for anyone to threaten you with harm."

"Oh, I'm sure your intentions were exactly the same as the caller's. In the long run, all you both want is for me to leave. I'm not going, Orville." She used his first name deliberately, refusing to use the title he'd denied her. "We can rip this valley apart with a fight or we can find some way to mend fences and agree to disagree. There's no need for you to dictate that your beliefs be imposed on my congregation."

She stood. "I will play this tape at the council meeting, if it becomes necessary. I can't imagine that many of the pastors in the valley would side with anyone who sounds this irrational and filled with hatred." She met his gaze evenly. "And it won't help your position that I'll be able to point out that you know exactly who made these calls."

An instant's shock spread over his face. "But that sounds very much like blackmail."

She managed a faint smile. "Why, yes, Orville, I believe it does."

With that, she walked out, leaving him to face the fact that she was willing to take him on in any type of fight he chose to wage—fair or otherwise. She just wished she felt a little better about her tactics.

It was another week before Richard found out about the upcoming council meeting. He heard about it not from Anna Louise, but straight from Orville Patterson. He should have suspected something the minute he walked into Patterson's for a quick cup of coffee and the whole place went quiet.

He spotted Orville sitting in a booth with Billy Joe Hunt and a couple of men he didn't recognize. The men suddenly seemed fascinated with their cups of coffee and cherry cokes from the fountain. Orville regarded him warily. There was an anticipatory gleam in Billy Joe Hunt's eyes that made Richard's heart pump a little faster.

Ignoring the lack of welcome, Richard pulled up a chair next to Orville and signaled to Tucker to bring over some coffee. "You all must be talking about Anna Louise," he said in a deceptively calm voice.

Orville remained tight-lipped, but Billy Joe wasn't smart enough to keep his mouth closed. "Yeah, I guess the preachers hereabouts will teach her a thing or two come next week."

"Meaning?"

"A woman don't belong behind the pulpit. Everybody knows that," Billy Joe said smugly.

Coming from anyone else, Richard would have dismissed Billy Joe's comment as yet another example of the small-minded stupidity one could expect to find in Kiley. He wouldn't have seen it as something worth fighting about. But this was Billy Joe and years of fury at the man's ignorance and cruel, senseless acts came bubbling to the surface.

He kept a tight rein on his temper, though. "You have something against the way Anna Louise has done her job?" he asked, his gaze pinned on Billy Joe. "You were there when we worked on the recreation hall. You saw how hard she worked."

"It's not personal," he declared staunchly, ignoring Orville's warning look. "And that didn't have nothing to do with the Church. She's just got no business standing up there on Sunday mornings preaching about sin and such. The Good Book says that's a man's job. What she's doing is blasphemy. Isn't that right?" He looked to Orville and the others for confirmation.

Something about his voice, his choice of words, caught Richard's attention. "Say that again."

"What's the matter, boy, can't you hear? The woman is defiling the church. Every word she speaks there is blasphemy, pure and simple." He again glanced toward Orville for approval. "Ain't that right?"

Orville avoided Billy Joe's question and Richard's increasingly furious gaze. With every fiber of his being, Richard wanted to reach into that booth and grab Billy Joe by his fat neck and strangle him, not for what he'd said just now to him, but for all the times he'd said the same thing to Anna Louise's answering machine.

He warned himself that Anna Louise wouldn't thank him for getting into a brawl on her behalf. He even tried to tell himself that it wasn't really his fight. And a few months ago, it might not have been.

But that was before he'd gotten to know Anna Louise, before he'd realized just how much her career meant to her and what it had already cost her to follow her calling. It was before he'd seen her take a whole community into her heart. It was before he'd listened to her preach, speaking the Word of God with an accuracy and a passion that touched the very souls of her congregation.

And it was before she'd opened her arms to one wayward, jaded journalist, expecting nothing in return, just welcoming him, believing in him and slowly filling his heart with hope.

It might not be his fight, but it was Anna Louise's and these days that amounted to the same thing. He turned his body until he could look Orville Patterson straight in the eye. Here was the real source of the conflict and the one man in a position to halt this absurd vendetta against Anna Louise.

"Is that the way you think, too?" he asked quietly.

Orville's expression hardened. "Stay out of it, Richard. You're just passing through."

The accusation stung, because until just this moment it had probably been true. Right now, though, he recognized that anywhere Anna Louise Perkins lived was home to him. Like it or not, he'd just have to figure some way to make it work. He regarded Orville—his closest childhood friend—with utter contempt.

"I never thought I'd live to say this," Richard told the man with whom he'd grown up and attended Sunday services for the first eighteen years of his life before he'd left Kiley and his faith behind. He cast a regretful look toward Tucker as he spoke, but he could see that Tucker was merely nodding encouragement.

Richard continued, "You're a fool, Orville, and this is one fight I intend to see that you lose. Before you take on Anna Louise, I'd suggest you go back and take a closer look at some of the Scripture you're always spouting. I seem to recall quite a bit that you've evidently forgotten."

He cited the pertinent passages, then stood and leaned over until he was in Billy Joe's face. "As for *you,* if you so much as dial Anna Louise's number again, you will have not only me, but the sheriff to deal with."

He allowed the threat to sink in, then nodded curtly. "Good day, gentlemen."

Not until he was back outside did he admit to himself what he'd done in Patterson's Drugstore and Soda Fountain. He'd drawn a battle line in public and placed himself squarely on the same side as Anna Louise. He stood right where he was for a minute and thought about the meaning of that. Slowly a grin spread across his face.

"Well, I'll be damned," he muttered. He wondered if Anna Louise would recognize it for the confession of love it was or if she'd just blast him for interfering.

Chapter Fifteen

Anna Louise heard about the argument Richard had had with Orville Patterson from half a dozen people before suppertime the same day. Several people called her at the church. Two more stopped her on the street. Maisey even managed to sneak out of ICU to get to a phone after Millicent reported the astonishing turn of events to her. She was clearly elated.

Even more amazing, Orville Patterson's daddy repeated every last word the men had spoken when Anna Louise stopped by the drugstore to pick up a prescription before going to call on a member of the congregation who lived alone and was down with the flu. Since Tucker Patterson told her with a grin on his face, she had to assume he'd taken Richard's side over his own son's.

At first she'd been alarmed when Tucker mentioned that Billy Joe Hunt had been there, but he'd reassured her that Richard had held his temper firmly in check.

"Did he realize—" She cut herself off, not wanting to get into the harassment issue with him.

"That Billy Joe was the one who'd been making those calls to you?" he asked, surprising her. "Yes, he figured that out straightaway. There was fire in his eyes, I'll tell you that, but he didn't strangle the man the way I was tempted to do. He just warned him that one more call would be the end of his sorry hide."

"Amazing," Anna Louise murmured, half to herself.

"When are you going to marry that young man and put him out of his misery?" Tucker had asked then.

"He hasn't asked."

"He will," Tucker said confidently. "You going to say yes?"

Anna Louise hadn't allowed herself to think that far into the future. She'd been trying too hard to convince herself to give up any hope of Richard making a commitment in their lifetimes. "I guess we'll see when the time comes," she told Tucker. "*If* it does."

When Anna Louise had finished her calls for the afternoon, she went looking for the man who'd stood up for her. Despite Tucker's interpretation, she wasn't sure what to make of what he'd done. The only way to understand it was to look him in the eye and ask.

Figuring that the unseasonably warm afternoon would have drawn him outdoors, she looked first out by Willow Creek. There was no sign of him. She finally found him in Maisey's apple orchard, sitting on a blanket that had been doubled up. He was propped up against a tree, wearing a heavy jacket, an old hat shading his eyes from the setting sun.

"Thank you," she said softly, dropping down beside him on the blanket that turned out to be scant protection from the cold, hard ground. One day of sixty-degree temperatures was no match for a winter's worth of icy weather.

"For what?"

"For standing up for me. You didn't have to, you know. I can fight my own battles. I've been doing it a long time now."

His blue eyes glinted back at her. "Maybe so, but I didn't see that I had much choice."

"Oh?"

"Orville was wrong and he was smug about it, to boot. No one I know has worked harder or been more dedicated to their beliefs than you. You don't just talk your principles, you live them every day of your life. As for Billy Joe, he's lucky I didn't strip him of his sorry hide."

Anna Louise drew in a sharp breath. "You figured it out, then? Tucker guessed you had."

"Figured out that Billy Joe was the one making the calls? Yes, I figured it out," he said mildly. "Apparently you did, too. Why didn't you mention it?"

She shrugged. "I didn't want to be the one responsible for your stripping him of his sorry hide."

"How very considerate," he commented dryly. "Were you thinking of him or me?"

"You, of course. And myself. I'd hate having to visit you in jail."

"I'm not the one who would have been sent to jail," he said with that supreme confidence she sometimes envied. "Besides, I have other fish to fry."

He tossed his hat aside and slanted a hot, hungry look at her that made her stomach do flip-flops. She couldn't think of a thing to say in response to his unspoken declaration of his wicked intentions. She'd promised herself she was going to forget about the desire she'd recognized in his eyes in the past. That promise kept her speechless. It didn't matter, because Richard seemed to have quite a bit on his mind.

"For instance," he continued. "I've been thinking I just might come back here permanently. That made this disagreement with Orville and Billy Joe a little more personal."

She regarded him in amazement. "You have? When did you decide that? I thought you hated it here."

"Things change," he said, his gaze pinned on her. "More importantly, I've changed."

Anna Louise's breath seemed to be caught in her throat. Was it possible that he was ready to let go of the past? She couldn't read his expression at all. Well, she could read that expression of longing plain as day, but she'd chosen to ignore that. "What are you saying?" she asked finally.

"Just that I'd sure hate to decide to stay here in Kiley when the woman I want as my wife is about to pack her bags and go off in search of another church. I figured I'd better do something to see that didn't happen."

So Tucker and Maisey were right, after all. Anna Louise couldn't have been more flabbergasted if Richard had announced he was going off to become a Buddhist monk.

Fighting to maintain a serious expression, when her heart seemed about to burst with pure joy, Anna Louise said, "So this argument you and Orville had was motivated by purely selfish reasons?"

"That it was," he said. A lazy, devastating grin spread across his face. "Is that a mortal sin?"

She gave the question the deliberation it deserved, then leaned down and kissed lips that were still warm from the last rays of the sun. When she lifted her head, the corners of his mouth tilted up.

"Now I know that *that* was a sin," he declared. "In fact, it was just about the sweetest sin I've ever committed. It could become downright addictive."

Anna Louise gazed into his warm, laughing eyes. "You're a fraud, Richard Walton."

His expression turned indignant. "Now that's a fine thing to be saying to the man who's just asked you to marry him."

"I don't recall hearing those precise words."

"And here I thought you were so intuitive. I intended to wait and do this up right, but here goes." He took her hand in his. His gaze locked with hers. "Anna Louise Perkins, would you do me the honor of becoming my wife?"

Anna Louise wasn't about to play coy. Richard was too darned slippery. He might wriggle off the hook. "How soon?"

He laughed at the quick response. "The minute you say yes."

"Yes," she said at once, leaning forward to kiss him again. "Yes, yes, yes."

But as happy as she was, Anna Louise was afraid that Richard was making a promise he wasn't ready to keep. "I can't believe you're ready to give up chasing stories around the globe," she said.

"I've been sitting here all afternoon giving that a lot of thought."

"And?"

Richard shrugged. "I'm not so sure my voice will ever effect any sort of change in places where people are intent on destroying each other. Here, though, I could start up a brand new paper and maybe make a difference. Maybe if enough people made the commitment just to try to change the world in their immediate vicinity, we could eventually fix up every single corner of the globe."

She was startled by his new sense of purpose and pleased by it. "You want to start a paper in Kiley? That would keep you happy?"

"I've got some money saved. It'd probably only be a weekly at first and it would probably have to serve the whole county, but who knows what I could make of it given time. If there had been a local paper around to cover this business between you and Orville, maybe it would never have gotten out of hand the way it has.

In fact, maybe I'll make that story the lead in my first edition."

"Great idea, except you won't be able to report it," she reminded him.

"Why the hell not?"

"Conflict of interest. Unless that proposal of yours was all talk."

"Definitely not." He grinned. "I knew you were going to have a positive influence on me."

"Your journalistic ethics were never in doubt."

"But in this one instance I might have been willing to bend them. Instead, I'll hire a free-lance person to write the story. The important thing is to rally public support in your favor."

Touched by his determination and the warmth shining in his eyes when he looked at her, Anna Louise knelt in front of him and framed his face with her hands. "I love you for wanting to do this, for wanting to sacrifice your career to stay here, but are you sure? Really sure?"

He nodded. "Thanks to you I've discovered that peace comes from knowing you've given life and love your best shot." He glanced at her. "What? You think there's more to it?"

Anna Louise nodded. "I understand why you were so hell-bent on leaving here in the first place. You haven't resolved that. Can you be truly happy coming back, if you haven't settled things with Billy Joe?"

"It's true that I grew up hating this town and its small-minded people," he admitted finally. "And if it hadn't been for my grandmother, I would never have come back."

Anna Louise's heart thudded dully. It wasn't over for him, at all. How could he possibly conceive of staying, even for her? How long would it take before he hated her for forcing him to make the choice?

"Those same people are here now," she reminded him. She knew the power of forgiveness, but she wasn't so sure that he did. "Can you let go of your bitterness toward them?"

He looked her in the eyes. "I'll be honest with you. It won't be easy. I doubt there will ever come a day when I'll be able to look Billy Joe in the face and not think about him causing my mother's death. Or about what he's been doing to you these past few months."

He reached for her hand and held it tight. "But I've been around the world. The people here are no better or worse than anywhere else. I've worked side-by-side with people in Kiley, thanks to you. Yes, a few of them may be intolerant and mean-spirited, but the only way to change that is to stay and fight. You've taught me that. If I'm only going to look for the bad in people, I'll find it anywhere. It's time I started seeing the good."

"And learned to forgive?"

He nodded. "And learned to forgive."

Anna Louise pressed her lips to his. "I love you, Richard Walton."

Richard sighed. "I love you, too, Anna Louise Perkins."

* * *

They set their wedding day for mid-April, to give
Richard a chance to get his new paper up and running, to give Maisey time to recuperate, which she was
suddenly determined to do one more time, and to allow Anna Louise to devote all of her energy to the upcoming meeting with the church council.

Not that she could concentrate worth a darn. She
finally understood exactly what she'd been asking of
Jeremy and Maribeth when she'd encouraged them to
postpone their wedding. Not a night went by that she
didn't toss and turn restlessly, longing for Richard's
touch, imagining her body twined with his. Not a day
went by that she didn't scandalize the whole town of
Kiley by kissing him soundly in public. If that was all
she could do before the wedding—and Richard was
sweetly adamant about that—then by heaven she was
going to enjoy it.

To be honest, it was astonishing how many nu-
ances a kiss could have. There were chaste pecks, limited to those times when they were subject to Millicent
Rawlings's disapproving frowns. There were teasing,
tantalizing kisses and hurried kisses, stolen whenever
they had the chance.

And then, of course, there were the deep, passion-
ate, breath-stealing kisses. Those were the ones that
almost destroyed Richard's resolve and turned Anna
Louise into a wreck. If they kept up those particular
kisses much longer, she was going to throw Richard to
the floor and have her way with him the second they
walked down the aisle as man and wife. Goodness, but

that man knew how to make an inexperienced woman feel like a regular siren.

She was thinking about just such a kiss on her doorstep the previous night—Richard flatly refused to be alone with her inside the house—when she realized that Orville Patterson had just addressed a remark to her. The most important meeting of her professional life and she'd been daydreaming like a smitten schoolgirl!

"What is it?" she said.

"Miss Perkins..."

"*Pastor* Perkins," she corrected automatically.

His jaw worked, but eventually he managed to grit out the words. "Pastor Perkins..."

"Thank you."

"I was just inquiring about your qualifications."

Anna Louise bit back a smile. Bad question, Orville, she thought. She laid out her course of studies in college, graduate school and seminary. "I believe that more than meets the necessary standards, doesn't it?" she said, trying very hard not to sound smug. She knew darn well it was more education than he had.

"Why, yes," he said.

She wondered what kind of man would start a fight like this without knowing such a simple thing about her background. Or maybe he'd hoped to scare her off long before it ever became an issue.

He turned to the other pastors who had gathered at the Jasper Junction church. "I believe we have no grounds to deny Miss—rather, Pastor Perkins the right to maintain her position in the Kiley church."

Anna Louise almost fell off her chair. Behind her, she heard Richard's indrawn breath.

Apparently the comment took the others by surprise, as well.

"Now wait just a minute here. Are you saying you're withdrawing your objections, Pastor Patterson?" one of the others asked. Anna Louise recognized him as Harlan Baskins, whom she knew to be as rigid and set in his ways as Orville.

Orville glanced at Richard, then met Anna Louise's gaze head-on. "I believe there is room to argue this on Scriptural grounds, but I will not fight the majority if it is your will to grant her the right to continue in her present position."

"But we haven't even voted yet. How do you know it's our will?" Harlan Baskins demanded, his flushed face a study in confusion. "What's going on here? Did a bunch of you cook up a deal?"

"Harlan, are you saying you still object?" the council chairman asked.

"Of course, I do."

"Well, then, perhaps, we should hear from Pastor Perkins." He looked to Anna Louise. "Do you feel there are legitimate grounds for a woman to hold the position you currently hold?"

"Absolutely," Anna Louise said. She stood and faced them. After a quick look in Richard's direction to draw on his strength, she took a deep breath and began. She started with what she knew from studying the Bible, then wound up with the way she'd been raised to believe that all of mankind had the right to strive for whatever goals were within their reach.

"There are those who've said I am bold or daring or courageous. There are some who've labeled me blasphemous. I want to reassure you about my motives and about how I see myself. I am not doing this to be controversial. Far from it, in fact. I'd like to be a simple, country preacher in a town I love," she said with heartfelt sincerity.

"Nor am I trying to be a trendsetter. I am just a woman whose faith is strong, whose sense of calling is powerful, whose desire to serve is built on an unconditional love of my God and my church. If you deny me the chance to fulfill the calling that has guided me for almost my entire life, then you will be denying me the opportunity to be myself. And worse, I sincerely believe you will be denying the people of my church in Kiley the right granted to every other church in our denomination, the right to select the pastor most suited to lead their congregation."

Her voice held steady as she looked directly into the eyes of each of these men—some old, like Harlan Baskins, some young, like Orville, some liberal, some conservative, all genuinely dedicated to the conviction that their way was right.

"It is not just my career," she said finally, "but my very life that is in your hands."

The words lingered in the air. Eventually the chairman cleared his throat and looked around the table. "Gentlemen, are there any questions or are you ready to vote?"

"I've heard enough. Let's get on with it," Harlan Baskins grumbled, glaring at Anna Louise. "Make her leave."

She faced the chairman. "I'd like to stay."

Pastor Baskins rose to his feet. "If she stays in this room, I will leave."

"Oh, sit down, Harlan," Orville snapped. "We all know how you're voting, so what's the point of hiding?"

After a bit more squabbling, they agreed to allow her to stay. They also insisted on a secret ballot, rather than a show of hands. When the chairman had all of the slips of paper, he began reading them off one by one.

"For approval," he said. "For approval."

Anna Louise's spirits began to lift. Then there were three consecutive votes against her. And another for.

In the end, the vote was nine to five in favor of allowing her to remain the pastor of the church in Kiley.

Tears clogged her throat. She could feel Richard's hand, warm and reassuring on her shoulder.

"Thank you," she said, her voice choked with emotion. Only then did she allow herself to admit exactly how terrified she had been that she might lose. Never once had she considered what she might do if that had happened.

"Thank you, gentlemen," she said one more time, then turned her gaze on Richard and tucked her arm through his. "Let's go plan a wedding."

Chapter Sixteen

Richard Walton and Anna Louise Perkins were married the last Saturday in April in the white clapboard church where Anna Louise was now the officially approved pastor. Huge straw baskets of daffodils, tulips and forsythia had been gathered for decoration. Sunlight streamed through the single stained-glass window above the altar.

The whole town turned out for the celebration. The nine pastors—out of fourteen from three counties—who'd voted to allow Anna Louise to remain on had been invited to conduct the wedding ceremony, each of them offering a prayer while one read the vows.

Best of all, Maisey, who had stubbornly rallied one more time, was there to see her grandson wed to a young woman she already loved as if she'd always been a part of her family. She'd spent the whole morning fussing over his suit and tie, until he was ready to scream. Then he recalled how terribly sad this day might have been if she hadn't lived to see it.

He had stilled her hands and kissed her forehead. "I love you, Grandmother."

"I know that, Richard. I always have. No woman could have asked for a finer grandson." A smile had spread across her face. "And now I'll have the prettiest granddaughter in the county, too. See to it you get busy on giving me some great-grandbabies right away."

"I'll do my best," he had promised.

Now he turned from his place in front of the altar and caught a glimpse of Maisey standing in the front pew, her posture erect, her face serene. She winked at him. Grinning, he winked back.

Then Mabel Hartley, decked out in a splashy print dress and, no doubt, another of her valiant girdles, struck the first chord of the wedding march. Instantly all of Richard's attention was riveted on the back of the church.

Anna Louise's sisters, all of them lovely, but not one a match for his beautiful bride, were serving as the bridesmaids. Two were currently married, but the oldest—Jane Ellen—had recently been divorced. There was an aura of sadness about her that made Richard wonder what some fool had done to her. He'd have to ask Anna Louise about that one of these days. He was actually looking forward to having a large extended family to worry about.

When all three sisters reached the front of the church, there was a faint hesitation in the music and then Anna Louise and her father stood framed in the doorway. Richard's breath caught in his throat at the sight of her in her simple, knee-length dress with her bouquet of apple blossoms. He couldn't help smiling at the memory of the first time he had set eyes on her in Maisey's orchard. She looked every bit as tempting now.

But after today, she would no longer be out of his reach. She would be his. He still couldn't quite believe his good fortune.

Anna Louise's vows were simple and heartfelt. And then it was Richard's turn. For a man who had built a career on weaving words into pictures, he had struggled for days to write these. Never had he found an assignment more difficult. Never had one mattered so much.

He looked into her upturned face and for a moment he forgot everything he had written. Then, at last, he remembered.

"Anna Louise, you have brought sunlight into my life where before there was only darkness. You have given me love and faith, strength and hope, four of the greatest gifts any human being can ever bestow on another. I hope that what I am able to give you in return is even half as meaningful."

He looked into brown eyes that glistened with unshed tears. "I give you my love, my devotion and my commitment for all the days of our life. I will be guided by your faith. I will be strengthened by your love. I will share your hope for a better world for all mankind and I will work in my own way to make that happen. I promise to love, honor and cherish you always."

When the pastor pronounced them man and wife, Anna Louise whispered, "I love you," just as his mouth touched hers. His whole body trembled with the force of his need for her.

At Maisey's suggestion the reception was held under the flowering apple trees in the Walton orchard. Picnic tables were laden with fried chicken, pork barbecue, potato salad, coleslaw and baked beans. A three-tiered wedding cake sat amid a dozen or more pies—mostly apple, baked with the last of last season's crop.

When everyone had been served, Anna Louise stood. "Let us pray." As heads bowed, she went on. "Thank you, our Heavenly Father, for letting us share this special day with family and friends. Thank you for all the blessings you have bestowed on us. Thank you for bringing into my life a man with a vision of the world as a better place and the courage to try to make that happen. With your guidance, perhaps all of us in Kiley will find our own ways to make his vision a reality. Thank you for our sense of community, which grows stronger each day, and thank you for allowing love to touch our lives. Amen."

Richard was startled to discover that Anna Louise's simple prayer had brought tears to eyes that had seen too much misery and unhappiness. He'd been so sure that nothing would ever touch him again. Anna

Louise, he knew, had never believed that for a minute. It was hard to remain jaded in the face of such optimism.

He wrapped his arms around her from behind and whispered in her ear. Startled eyes met his.

"We haven't even cut the cake," she protested.

"Are you sure that's a requirement?"

"Absolutely." Mischief danced in her eyes. "I'll make the wait worth your while."

He grinned slowly. "It's been a *very* long wait," he reminded her.

"Are you suggesting I'm not up to the task?"

He shook his head, laughing at her indignation. "No, my beautiful bride. I'm just suggesting that it will take more than one night, maybe even more than a year of nights to make up for the torment you've put me through."

"Nobility does have its price, doesn't it?" she teased.

Richard had wanted to show Anna Louise Paris or Rome or London. He had offered her an island in the Caribbean or a beach in Tahiti for their honeymoon. But Anna Louise had held out for a week in a cabin in the Smoky Mountains, far from the cares of the rest of the world.

She drew in a deep breath as she gazed into the steamy bathroom mirror, studying her reflection and wondering at the sudden transformation she found there. She had always thought of herself as ordinary. She had convinced herself that Richard Walton was the only man on earth who imagined her beautiful. Tonight, though, she could almost see it and she gave all the credit to her love for the man waiting for her in the cabin's bedroom. He had brought the color to her cheeks, the glow to her eyes.

She touched the daring, filmy negligee that her sisters had insisted she have for her wedding night. Obviously they'd feared she'd choose flannel. The lace trim of this one was French and as delicate as a spider's web. She wondered how long it would last under Richard's anxious caresses and laughed at the folly of putting it on at all. Then, again, wedding nights were all about romance and she had never in her life felt more romantic.

When she finally opened the door, she found the bedroom dark except for the light from the fireplace, where Richard had set a blaze earlier. He was sitting in a chair beside the hearth, waiting, his gaze pinned on her. Slowly, he stood.

"You were right," he said, his voice hushed.

"About what?"

"This was worth waiting for."

Anna Louise felt her pulse leap and her skin heat at the unmistakable anticipation in his voice. When he started toward her, her heart thundered in her chest. And as he scooped her into his arms and held her against his bare chest, she wondered anew at the willpower it had taken for them to wait so long for this moment.

She wanted to discover everything about him. She needed to know how he would taste, how his skin would heat when she touched him, how he would feel inside her. The urgency to know all of that almost overwhelmed her. She buried her face against his neck, savoring the fresh, soapy scent of his skin, the sudden warming of his flesh beneath her lips. He groaned as she peppered kisses across his shoulder.

"Slow down, sweetheart. I'm already burning up," he warned.

"I need you," she whispered. "There are so many things I've imagined doing with you, so many times when I've imagined your touch. I want to know if I was right."

Heat blazed in his eyes. "Do you want me to turn this over to you, then? I'm willing to let you experiment to your heart's content."

It was an intriguing thought. It took some of the unspoken fear out of what was to happen between them. "Really?"

He settled her on the bed, then stretched out next to her, still wearing a pair of jeans and nothing more. "I'm all yours," he said generously, his expression wickedly sensual.

Anna Louise knew at least that his jaw was almost never without a faint hint of stubble, but she traced it with her fingertips, anyway. It was smoothly shaven, but the texture was still obviously masculine.

She outlined his lips—his dear, familiar, provocative lips—and dared to slant her mouth over his. The most daring kiss they'd ever shared was nothing compared to the darkly sensual allure of this one, which for the first time was a prelude rather than an end unto itself. She relished the minty taste of his mouth, savored the swirling touch of his tongue and allowed her body to flow with the sensations the kiss aroused.

She could have tarried over that kiss for an eternity, it seemed, but there was so much more. Her fingers smoothed over the curling hairs on his chest. Her lips found a masculine nipple to tease. There was his flat stomach to trace until her hand reached the waistband of his jeans and came to a halt.

Her gaze caught his and held as she worked the button open, then snagged the tab of the zipper and slowly eased it down, her knuckles trailing along the bare flesh beneath. Her heart hammered in her chest when she first touched the heated silk of his arousal. Still looking into his eyes, dark with desire, she felt the power and desperation of their shared longing and she trembled violently.

"I need you now," she whispered, suddenly filled with uncertainty and needing his experience to carry them over what was, to her, terrifyingly unfamiliar terrain.

She expected him to shed his jeans first, but instead he lifted a hand to caress her cheek. He pulled her down until she was lying atop him, aware of every hard, masculine inch of him. Then he delicately kissed her eyelids, her nose, her mouth. Sparks of yearning danced through her, building as he finally swept his hands over her breasts, teasing her nipples through the filmy material that only accentuated his touches.

Anna Louise felt as if she were floating on a sea of sensation, comforting at first, but now beginning to turn tumultuous as his caresses became increasingly intimate. Her gown came up, lifted by a caress that left a trail of fire along her thigh. Never had she imagined that it would be like this. Never had she thought that the love between a man and a woman could make every fiber of her body feel so vibrantly alive. It was as if she'd been sleepwalking and now she was totally, magically awake.

Then her gown was tossed aside, along with Richard's jeans. He positioned himself above her, then hesitated.

"I want so much for this to be perfect for you," he whispered.

"It already is."

"But..."

"I know," she said, to reassure him that whatever pain there was to be was expected and would be forgotten in heartbeat. "Please."

Sweat beaded across his brow as he slowly, carefully, began to enter her, joining his hardness with her softness in a union that was as old as time. Her hips rose to meet each tentative thrust, her body anxious to discover where these sweet waves of sensation were leading. Then there was the quick, burning pain, followed by a sense of absolute completion, of unity.

Once again, that powerful urgency began to build as Richard moved inside her. Anna Louise felt herself floating toward some radiant place of unparalleled joy and when she found it, it was as if it splintered apart into a thousand rays of brilliant, incomparable light.

She felt Richard's muscles straining toward the same astonishing release and with bold touches she urged him on until his body rocked with a violent, shattering climax that matched her own.

"Dear Heaven," he murmured eventually, his voice husky, his breathing still uneven. He looked down at her and wiped a stray curl away from her cheek. "You're okay?"

"I have never felt like this before in my life."

A possessive smile spread across his face. "I should hope not."

"No doubt you have." The words were teasing, but she wasn't sure she'd been able to hide a trace of uncertainty.

"Never," he told her. "In my entire life, I have *never* experienced anything like what we just shared. Do you know why?"

"Why?" she asked, longing for the reassurance.

"Because love makes all the difference. I'll be the first to admit, I didn't think that was possible, but it's true. Knowing that, I wonder if I'll ever stop aching with need for you."

She slid her arms around his waist and touched her lips to his chest. "I will make you a promise right here and now, Richard Walton. I will be here for you whenever you need me, whenever you want me."

He regarded her seriously. "I'm glad we waited for this moment, Anna Louise."

"Why?"

"Because if we are together for a hundred years, this night is something I will never forget. I will always remember how willingly you gave yourself to me, how much wonder your touch inspired.''

Anna Louise sighed, her breath whispering against his bare skin. This was what it was all about, she thought as she drifted asleep for the first time in her husband's arms—the wonder of love.

* * * * *

A Note from the Author

From the moment I read an article in the *Los Angeles Times* about the struggles of women in the ministry, I began to envision a heroine with such strength of purpose, grace, wisdom and compassion. The daring, courageous women who choose this course must have bountiful faith to withstand the tests they will face during their careers. In Anna Louise Perkins, I hope I have created such a woman, the epitome of a Silhouette Special Woman.

Every woman, whether the road she chooses is dangerous, daring or the well-worn footpath of others who have gone before, must have the courage of her convictions. There will always be those who question her choice, but she is the only one whose opinion really matters.

''To thine own self be true.'' Those are the words today's women must live by. That is what makes each of us unique, *special women*. It's also what captivates the heart of that special man.

Wishing you wisdom, courage and self-knowledge.

Dark secrets, dangerous desire...

Lovers
DARK AND
DANGEROUS

Three spine-tingling tales from the dark side of love.

This October, enter the world of shadowy romance as Silhouette presents the third in their annual tradition of thrilling love stories and chilling story lines. Written by three of Silhouette's top names:

LINDSAY McKENNA
LEE KARR
RACHEL LEE

Haunting a store near you this October.

Only from

Silhouette®

...where passion lives.

Silhouette ROMANCE™

First comes marriage.... Will love follow?
Find out this September when Silhouette Romance presents

Join six couples who marry for convenient reasons, and still find happily-ever-afters. Look for these wonderful books by some of your favorite authors:

#1030 *Timely Matrimony* by Kasey Michaels

#1031 *McCullough's Bride* by Anne Peters

#1032 *One of a Kind Marriage* by Cathie Linz

#1033 *Oh, Baby!* by Lauryn Chandler

#1034 *Temporary Groom* by Jayne Addison

#1035 *Wife in Name Only* by Carolyn Zane

JINGLE BELLS, WEDDING BELLS:
Silhouette's Christmas Collection for 1994

Christmas Wish List

*To beat the crowds at the malls and get the perfect present for *everyone,* even that snoopy Mrs. Smith next door!

*To get through the holiday parties without running my panty hose.

*To bake cookies, decorate the house and serve the perfect Christmas dinner—just like the women in all those magazines.

*To sit down, curl up and read my Silhouette Christmas stories!

Join *New York Times* bestselling author Nora Roberts, along with popular writers Barbara Boswell, Myrna Temte and Elizabeth August, as we celebrate the joys of Christmas—and the magic of marriage—with

JINGLE BELLS, WEDDING BELLS

Silhouette's Christmas Collection for 1994.